Bedtime for Stories Stressed Out Adults

D1343411

Bedtime Stories for Stressed Out Adults

Tales to Soothe Tired Souls

Introduced by
LUCY MANGAN

HODDER &
STOUGHTON

First published in Great Britain in 2018 by Hodder & Stoughton
An Hachette UK company

1

Introduction © Lucy Mangan 2018

A CIP catalogue record for this title is available from the British Library

Hardback ISBN 978 1 473 69591 7
Trade Paperback ISBN 978 1 473 69590 0
eBook ISBN 978 1 473 69589 4

Typeset in Sabon MT by Hewer Text UK Ltd, Edinburgh
Printed and bound by CPI Group (UK) Ltd, Croydon CRO 4YY

Hodder & Stoughton policy is to use papers that are natural, renewable
and recyclable products and made from wood grown in sustainable
forests. The logging and manufacturing processes are expected to
conform to the environmental regulations of the country of origin.

Hodder & Stoughton Ltd
Carmelite House
50 Victoria Embankment
London EC4Y 0DZ

www.hodder.co.uk

Table of Contents

Introduction by Lucy Mangan

Do you remember what it was like to read as a child? That blissful ease of total absorption in a book. The seamless slipping from reality to imagination. Sitting on the sofa as Cair Paravel, forgotten gardens, sea-bound Canadian provinces, bracken-filled moors, mysterious ruins, Minnesotan prairies and Swiss mountain ranges sprang up around you, and you accompanied red-haired heroines, loyal dogs, talking lions, ghosts, witches and children just like you but without the misfortune to be born in the dull here and duller now on their adventures until you were recalled to domesticity by the announcement of another mealtime, or bed.

I remember it well and would do much to recapture it. But not quite as much, perhaps, as I would do to recapture the similarly blissful ease of childhood sleep. I may have hated actually going to bed – meal calls were fine but this I dreaded, for who knew what fun the grown-ups were going to have without me! – but once I was there, the bountiful peace and warmth quickly overwhelmed me and I slipped as seamlessly as I had from Catford to

I

Miss Cackle's Academy from the waking world to the land of Morpheus.

Like most things in this life, the joy of sound sleep and immersive reading is wasted on the young. It's now, as adults that we really need all the restorative comforts they offer. Imagine a world in which you went to bed and . . . slept. Just . . . slept. Without lying there for an hour running through the day's events – perhaps updating the tally on your mental scorecard for personal success and failure (I subdivide mine into 'professional', 'domestic', 'maternal' and 'daughterly' categories for ease of access and more specific inner beratings; I am after all very busy. I don't have time for a scattergun approach to self-excoriation) – and vowing to do better tomorrow. Without the need to plan the next day's to-do list, map out a plan for the week and check it against the monthly planner in your mind (why don't you keep a notebook by the bed! screams your unforgiving inner critic, notching up another mark on the domestic failures board). Without running through the list of minor and major worries (from the ailing dishwasher, through to global warming and ending, always, on cancer) before finally falling asleep from sheer emotional exhaustion.

Imagine reading a book without a similar list of responsibilities crowding the words out of your brain, without a tide of anxiety pulling down the fictional world as fast as you try to build it.

This book is a small attempt to recreate these lost joys for – as the title says – stressed out adults, driven mad by the demands of home, family, work and the hopelessly porous boundary between all three. Which is floodlit, of course, by the cold blue light of the smartphone screen that somehow, despite our best efforts, seems to be the first thing we reach for in the morning and the last thing we scroll through – why? Why do we do it to ourselves? Why?! – at night. This collection of short stories (or nuggets mined from longer books because they similarly comprise a tale in miniature) and poems in this volume aim to dam for a little while the cross-currents of demand flowing endlessly through modern life and restore a little bit of peace to the end of our increasingly long and furious days.

Let the rhythms of the poems lull you ('So shut your eyes while Mother sings / Of wonderful sights that be, / And you shall see the beautiful things / As you rock in the misty sea / Where the old shoe rocked the fishermen three: – / Wynken, / Blynken, / And Nod.'), let the rest carry you off in their different ways. The elemental power of a fairy tale like *East of the Sun, West of the Moon* works on all of us at a visceral level – there are few worries and niggling irritations that can resist its insistent tug – though my own great love will always be the allied genre of myth, here beautifully represented by Andrew Lang's retelling of the most potent moment of them all; Arthur's revelation as the true born King, in *The Drawing of the Sword*. I would like to fall asleep every night hoping that the legend is true, and that he will come again to save us at our darkest hour. Which, metaphorically if not literally, by the way is four o'clock in the morning, as anyone who has ever – through bad luck, booze or newborn babe – been awake at that time knows.

Or of course, there is the common route out of the daily grind for us all; retracing our childhood steps. Even if you can't read quite as a child again, you can get close by reading *what* you read as a child again. So herein lies E. Nesbit's *The Aunt and Amabel*, whose disgraced young heroine goes through a wardrobe (and why not let this distract you with memories of other wardrobe-portals you have read, known and loved? It beats filling your mind with rage about the upcoming tube strike, need to make a costume for the next National Day of Needless Nonsense at school or inability of husbands to change the toilet roll) and finds both sympathy and redemption. Or you can revisit Heidi feasting on smoked meat and goat's cheese with grandfather in his hut, accompany Anne of Green Gables and Diana on their trip to see an Exhibition in town and home again, or head for the hidden corners of Misselthwaite Manor with Mary and Dickon and let the magical peace of *The Secret Garden* work on you once more. With any luck, you will soon find yourself tumbling like Alice, who also makes an appearance here, down the rabbit hole of consciousness, though hopefully exiting into a less wildly energetic dreamscape than Lewis Carroll constructed for his girl.

If childhood is not a place to flee to, or pure escapism simply not your thing – *Bedtime Stories* still has you covered. For grown-up fare and the adult comfort of a shared fate rather than a retreat, look to *The Tiredness of Rosabel*, as she replays the day's events at the shop in which she works over in her mind, amending and improving as she goes before finally drifting off to what promises to be at least temporarily restorative sleep. Or let the abdication of responsibility and the fugue state into which the penurious protagonist and mother of four in *A Pair of Silk*

Stockings descends induce the same in you for the few glorious minutes it takes to read her quietly subversive tale.

Individual tastes differ, of course, but every short story – whether in prose, poetry or mined from a larger piece – in here is, in two important ways, perfect bedtime fare. Why? Because they're short, and we're tired; and because they're stories.

Whatever age we are, stories soothe us. Stories are what psychologists call 'a primary act of mind'. In other words, formulating narratives is how we make sense of the world. We are not designed to experience life as a random series of discrete events acting upon us. If we habitually conceptualised ourselves as just another set of data points in an uncaring universe (though this brutal truth does seem to have a habit of uncovering itself at the aforementioned four o'clock in the morning), we would go mad. So we make connections, infer causality, predict, impute, anecdotalise – and cope.

Deliberately fashioned stories, laboured over, planed, polished to perfection go one better and provide us with narrative satisfaction and neat closure that life, despite our best efforts, rarely furnishes forth. Those in this book do so within a few pages, or verses. I defy anyone to close the cover on the delicately wrought lifecycle of Oscar Wilde's *Selfish Giant*, the shining rigour of Laura E. Richards' *The Golden Windows* or O. Henry's masterpiece *The Gift of the Magi* (the latter of whose especially precision-tooled parts come together and purr like a Rolls Royce engine) without a deep, deep sigh of utter contentment.

At an age at which existence generally seems defined – or at least circumscribed – by the number of things left undone (that to-do list never quite gets finished, larger jobs sit and fester like the gunk in the ailing dishwasher because calling the plumber is still on the to-do list, and – worst of all – older friends tell me that, despite my hopes, it never will feel like this parenting thing is a task completed, even if not well), what better way to end the day than with a tale consumed entire? Escape, and then end on a solid, real-life achievement.

Enjoy whichever tale you choose. May we all wynken, blynken and nod well tonight.

The Gift of the Magi

O. HENRY

One dollar and eighty-seven cents. That was all. And sixty
cents of it was in pennies. Pennies saved one and two at a
time by bulldozing the grocer and the vegetable man and the
butcher until one's cheeks burned with the silent imputation of
parsimony that such close dealing implied. Three times Della
counted it. One dollar and eighty-seven cents. And the next day
would be Christmas.

There was clearly nothing to do but flop down on the shabby
little couch and howl. So Della did it. Which instigates the moral
reflection that life is made up of sobs, sniffles, and smiles, with
sniffles predominating.

While the mistress of the home is gradually subsiding from
the first stage to the second, take a look at the home. A furnished
flat at $8 per week. It did not exactly beggar description, but it
certainly had that word on the lookout for the mendicancy
squad.

In the vestibule below was a letter-box into which no letter
would go, and an electric button from which no mortal finger

could coax a ring. Also appertaining thereunto was a card bearing the name 'Mr James Dillingham Young.'

The 'Dillingham' had been flung to the breeze during a former period of prosperity when its possessor was being paid $30 per week. Now, when the income was shrunk to $20, though, they were thinking seriously of contracting to a modest and unassuming D. But whenever Mr James Dillingham Young came home and reached his flat above he was called 'Jim' and greatly hugged by Mrs James Dillingham Young, already introduced to you as Della. Which is all very good.

Della finished her cry and attended to her cheeks with the powder rag. She stood by the window and looked out dully at a grey cat walking a grey fence in a grey backyard. Tomorrow would be Christmas Day, and she had only $1.87 with which to buy Jim a present. She had been saving every penny she could for months, with this result. Twenty dollars a week doesn't go far. Expenses had been greater than she had calculated. They always are. Only $1.87 to buy a present for Jim. Her Jim. Many a happy hour she had spent planning for something nice for him. Something fine and rare and sterling—something just a little bit near to being worthy of the honour of being owned by Jim.

There was a pier glass between the windows of the room. Perhaps you have seen a pier glass in an $8 flat. A very thin and very agile person may, by observing his reflection in a rapid sequence of longitudinal strips, obtain a fairly accurate conception of his looks. Della, being slender, had mastered the art.

Suddenly she whirled from the window and stood before the glass. Her eyes were shining brilliantly, but her face had lost its colour within twenty seconds. Rapidly she pulled down her hair and let it fall to its full length.

Now, there were two possessions of the James Dillingham Youngs in which they both took a mighty pride. One was Jim's gold watch that had been his father's and his grandfather's. The other was Della's hair. Had the queen of Sheba lived in the flat across the airshaft, Della would have let her hair hang out the window some day to dry just to depreciate Her Majesty's jewels and gifts. Had King Solomon been the janitor, with all his treasures piled up in the basement, Jim would have pulled out his watch every time he passed, just to see him pluck at his beard from envy.

So now Della's beautiful hair fell about her rippling and shining like a cascade of brown waters. It reached below her knee and made itself almost a garment for her. And then she did it up again nervously and quickly. Once she faltered for a minute and stood still while a tear or two splashed on the worn red carpet.

On went her old brown jacket; on went her old brown hat. With a whirl of skirts and with the brilliant sparkle still in her eyes, she fluttered out the door and down the stairs to the street.

Where she stopped the sign read: 'Mme Sofronie. Hair Goods of All Kinds.' One flight up Della ran, and collected herself, panting. Madame, large, too white, chilly, hardly looked the 'Sofronie'.

'Will you buy my hair?' asked Della.

'I buy hair,' said Madame. 'Take yer hat off and let's have a sight at the looks of it.'

Down rippled the brown cascade.

'Twenty dollars,' said Madame, lifting the mass with a practised hand.

'Give it to me quick,' said Della.

Oh, and the next two hours tripped by on rosy wings. Forget the hashed metaphor. She was ransacking the stores for Jim's present.

She found it at last. It surely had been made for Jim and no one else. There was no other like it in any of the stores, and she had turned all of them inside out. It was a platinum fob chain simple and chaste in design, properly proclaiming its value by substance alone and not by meretricious ornamentation – as all good things should do. It was even worthy of The Watch. As soon as she saw it she knew that it must be Jim's. It was like him. Quietness and value – the description applied to both. Twenty-one dollars they took from her for it, and she hurried home with the eighty-seven cents. With that chain on his watch Jim might be properly anxious about the time in any company. Grand as the watch was, he sometimes looked at it on the sly on account of the old leather strap that he used in place of a chain.

When Della reached home her intoxication gave way a little to prudence and reason. She got out her curling irons and lighted the gas and went to work repairing the ravages made by generosity added to love. Which is always a tremendous task, dear friends – a mammoth task.

Within forty minutes her head was covered with tiny, close-lying curls that made her look wonderfully like a truant schoolboy. She looked at her reflection in the mirror long, carefully, and critically.

'If Jim doesn't kill me,' she said to herself, 'before he takes a second look at me, he'll say I look like a Coney Island chorus girl. But what could I do – oh! what could I do with a dollar and eighty-seven cents?'

At seven o'clock the coffee was made and the frying-pan was on the back of the stove, hot and ready to cook the chops.

Jim was never late. Della doubled the fob chain in her hand and sat on the corner of the table near the door that he always entered. Then she heard his step on the stair away down on the first flight, and she turned white for just a moment. She had a habit of saying a little silent prayer about the simplest everyday things, and now she whispered: 'Please God, make him think I am still pretty.'

The door opened and Jim stepped in and closed it. He looked thin and very serious. Poor fellow, he was only twenty-two – and to be burdened with a family! He needed a new overcoat and he was without gloves.

Jim stopped inside the door, as immovable as a setter at the scent of quail. His eyes were fixed upon Della, and there was an expression in them that she could not read, and it terrified her. It was not anger, nor surprise, nor disapproval, nor horror, nor any of the sentiments that she had been prepared for. He simply stared at her fixedly with that peculiar expression on his face.

Della wriggled off the table and went for him.

'Jim, darling,' she cried, 'don't look at me that way. I had my hair cut off and sold because I couldn't have lived through Christmas without giving you a present. It'll grow out again – you won't mind, will you? I just had to do it. My hair grows awfully fast. Say "Merry Christmas!" Jim, and let's be happy. You don't know what a nice – what a beautiful, nice gift I've got for you.'

'You've cut off your hair?' asked Jim, laboriously, as if he had not arrived at that patent fact yet even after the hardest mental labour.

'Cut it off and sold it,' said Della. 'Don't you like me just as well, anyhow? I'm me without my hair, ain't I?'

Jim looked about the room curiously.

'You say your hair is gone?' he said, with an air almost of idiocy.

'You needn't look for it,' said Della. 'It's sold, I tell you – sold and gone, too. It's Christmas Eve, boy. Be good to me, for it went for you. Maybe the hairs of my head were numbered,' she went on with sudden serious sweetness, 'but nobody could ever count my love for you. Shall I put the chops on, Jim?'

Out of his trance Jim seemed quickly to wake. He enfolded his Della. For ten seconds let us regard with discreet scrutiny some inconsequential object in the other direction. Eight dollars a week or a million a year – what is the difference? A mathematician or a wit would give you the wrong answer. The magi brought valuable gifts, but that was not among them. This dark assertion will be illuminated later on.

Jim drew a package from his overcoat pocket and threw it upon the table.

'Don't make any mistake, Dell,' he said, 'about me. I don't think there's anything in the way of a haircut or a shave or a shampoo that could make me like my girl any less. But if you'll unwrap that package you may see why you had me going a while at first.'

White fingers and nimble tore at the string and paper. And then an ecstatic scream of joy; and then, alas! a quick feminine change to hysterical tears and wails, necessitating the immediate employment of all the comforting powers of the lord of the flat.

For there lay The Combs – the set of combs, side and back, that Della had worshipped long in a Broadway window. Beautiful combs, pure tortoise shell, with jewelled rims – just the shade to wear in the beautiful vanished hair. They were expensive combs, she knew, and her heart had simply craved and yearned over them without the least hope of possession. And now, they were hers, but the tresses that should have adorned the coveted adornments were gone.

But she hugged them to her bosom, and at length she was able to look up with dim eyes and a smile and say: 'My hair grows so fast, Jim!'

And then Della leaped up like a little singed cat and cried, 'Oh, oh!'

Jim had not yet seen his beautiful present. She held it out to him eagerly upon her open palm. The dull precious metal seemed to flash with a reflection of her bright and ardent spirit.

'Isn't it a dandy, Jim? I hunted all over town to find it. You'll have to look at the time a hundred times a day now. Give me your watch. I want to see how it looks on it.'

Instead of obeying, Jim tumbled down on the couch and put his hands under the back of his head and smiled.

'Dell,' said he, 'let's put our Christmas presents away and keep 'em a while. They're too nice to use just at present. I sold the watch to get the money to buy your combs. And now suppose you put the chops on.'

The magi, as you know, were wise men – wonderfully wise men – who brought gifts to the Babe in the manger. They invented the art of giving Christmas presents. Being wise, their gifts were no doubt wise ones, possibly bearing the privilege of exchange in case of duplication. And here I have lamely related to you the uneventful chronicle of two foolish children in a flat who most unwisely sacrificed for each other the greatest treasures of their house. But in a last word to the wise of these days let it be said that of all who give gifts these two were the wisest. Of all who give and receive gifts, such as they are wisest. Everywhere they are wisest. They are the magi.

The Mouse

SAKI

Theodoric Voler had been brought up, from infancy to the confines of middle age, by a fond mother whose chief solicitude had been to keep him screened from what she called the coarser realities of life. When she died she left Theodoric alone in a world that was as real as ever, and a good deal coarser than he considered it had any need to be. To a man of his temperament and upbringing even a simple railway journey was crammed with petty annoyances and minor discords, and as he settled himself down in a second-class compartment one September morning he was conscious of ruffled feelings and general mental discomposure.

He had been staying at a country vicarage, the inmates of which had been certainly neither brutal nor bacchanalian, but their supervision of the domestic establishment had been of that lax order which invites disaster. The pony carriage that was to take him to the station had never been properly ordered, and when the moment for his departure drew near, the handyman who should have produced the required article was nowhere to be found. In this emergency Theodoric, to his mute but very intense disgust, found himself obliged to collaborate with the vicar's daughter in the task of harnessing the pony, which necessitated groping about in an ill-lighted outbuilding called a stable, and smelling very like one – except in patches where it smelled of mice. Without being actually afraid of mice, Theodoric classed them among the coarser incidents of life, and considered that Providence, with a little exercise of moral courage, might long ago have recognised that they were not indispensable, and have withdrawn them from circulation.

As the train glided out of the station Theodoric's nervous imagination accused himself of exhaling a weak odour of stable yard, and possibly of displaying a mouldy straw or two on his unusually well-brushed garments. Fortunately the only other occupation of the compartment, a lady of about the same age as himself, seemed inclined for slumber rather than scrutiny; the train was not due to stop till the terminus was reached, in about an hour's time, and the carriage was of the old-fashioned sort that held no communication with a corridor, therefore no further travelling companions were likely to intrude on Theodoric's semiprivacy. And yet the train had scarcely attained its normal speed before he became reluctantly but vividly aware that he was not alone with the slumbering lady; he was not even alone in his own clothes.

A warm, creeping movement over his flesh betrayed the unwelcome and highly resented presence, unseen but poignant, of a strayed mouse, that had evidently dashed into its present retreat during the episode of the pony harnessing. Furtive stamps and shakes and wildly directed pinches failed to dislodge the intruder, whose motto, indeed, seemed to be Excelsior; and the lawful occupant of the clothes lay back against the cushions and endeavoured rapidly to evolve some means for putting an end to the dual ownership. It was unthinkable that he should continue for the space of a whole hour in the horrible position of a Rowton House for vagrant mice (already his imagination had at least doubled the numbers of the alien invasion). On the other hand, nothing less drastic than partial disrobing would ease him of his tormentor, and to undress in the presence of a lady, even for so laudable a purpose, was an idea that made his ear tips tingle in a blush of abject shame. He had never been able to bring himself even to the mild exposure of open-work socks in the presence of the fair sex. And yet – the lady in this case was to all appearances soundly and securely asleep; the mouse, on the other hand, seemed to be trying to crowd a wanderjahr into a few strenuous minutes. If there is any truth in the theory of transmigration, this particular mouse must certainly have been in a former state a member of the Alpine Club. Sometimes in its eagerness it lost its footing and slipped for half an inch or so; and then, in fright, or more probably temper, it bit. Theodoric was goaded into the most audacious undertaking of his life. Crimsoning to the hue of a beetroot and keeping an agonised watch on his slumbering fellow traveller, he swiftly and noiselessly secured the ends of his railway rug to the racks on either side of the carriage, so that a substantial curtain hung athwart the compartment. In the narrow dressing room that he had thus improvised he proceeded with violent haste to extricate himself partially and the mouse entirely from the surrounding casings of tweed and half-wool.

As the unravelled mouse gave a wild leap to the floor, the rug, slipping its fastening at either end, also came down with a heart-curdling flop, and almost simultaneously the awakened sleeper opened her eyes. With a movement almost quicker than the mouse's, Theodoric pounced on the rug and hauled its ample folds chin-high over his dismantled person as he collapsed into the farther corner of the carriage. The blood raced and beat in the veins of his neck and forehead, while he waited dumbly for the communication cord to be pulled. The lady, however, contented herself with a silent stare at her strangely muffled companion. How much had she seen, Theodoric queried to himself; and in any case what on earth must she think of his present posture?

'I think I have caught a chill,' he ventured desperately.

'Really, I'm sorry,' she replied. 'I was just going to ask you if you would open this window.'

'I fancy it's malaria,' he added, his teeth chattering slightly, as much from fright as from a desire to support his theory.

'I've got some brandy in my holdall, if you'll kindly reach it down for me,' said his companion.

'Not for worlds – I mean, I never take anything for it,' he assured her earnestly.

'I suppose you caught it in the tropics?'

Theodoric, whose acquaintance with the tropics was limited to an annual present of a chest of tea from an uncle in Ceylon, felt that even the malaria was slipping from him. Would it be possible, he wondered, to disclose the real state of affairs to her in small instalments?

'Are you afraid of mice?' he ventured, growing, if possible, more scarlet in the face.

'Not unless they came in quantities. Why do you ask?'

'I had one crawling inside my clothes just now,' said Theodoric in a voice that hardly seemed his own. 'It was a most awkward situation.'

'It must have been, if you wear your clothes at all tight,' she observed. 'But mice have strange ideas of comfort.'

'I had to get rid of it while you were asleep,' he continued. Then, with a gulp, he added, 'It was getting rid of it that brought me to – to this.'

'Surely leaving off one small mouse wouldn't bring on a chill,' she exclaimed, with a levity that Theodoric accounted abominable.

Evidently she had detected something of his predicament, and was enjoying his confusion. All the blood in his body seemed to have mobilised in one concentrated blush, and an agony of abasement, worse than a myriad mice, crept up and down over his soul. And then, as reflection began to assert itself, sheer terror took the place of humiliation. With every minute that passed the train was rushing nearer to the crowded and bustling terminus, where dozens of prying eyes would be exchanged for the one paralysing pair that watched him from the farther corner of the carriage. There was one slender, despairing chance, which the next few minutes must decide. His fellow traveller might relapse into a blessed slumber. But as the minutes throbbed by that chance ebbed away. The furtive glance which Theodoric stole at her from time to time disclosed only an unwinking wakefulness.

'I think we must be getting near now,' she presently observed.

Theodoric had already noted with growing terror the recurring stacks of small, ugly dwellings that heralded the journey's end. The words acted as a signal. Like a hunted beast breaking cover and dashing madly toward some other haven of momentary safety he threw aside his rug, and struggled frantically into his dishevelled garments. He was conscious of dull suburban stations racing past the window, of a choking, hammering sensation in his throat and heart, and of an icy silence in that corner toward which he dared not look. Then as he sank back in his seat, clothed and almost delirious, the train slowed down to a final crawl, and the woman spoke.

'Would you be so kind,' she asked, 'as to get me a porter to put me into a cab? It's a shame to trouble you when you're feeling unwell, but being blind makes one so helpless at a railway station.'

East of the Sun, West of the Moon

ANDREW LANG

Once upon a time there was a poor husbandman who had many children and little to give them in the way either of food or clothing. They were all pretty, but the prettiest of all was the youngest daughter, who was so beautiful that there were no bounds to her beauty.

So once – it was late on a Thursday evening in autumn, and wild weather outside, terribly dark, and raining so heavily and blowing so hard that the walls of the cottage shook again – they were all sitting together by the fireside, each of them busy with something or other, when suddenly someone rapped three times against the window-pane. The man went out to see what could be the matter, and when he got out there stood a great big white bear.

'Good-evening to you,' said the White Bear.

'Good-evening,' said the man.

'Will you give me your youngest daughter?' said the White Bear; 'if you will, you shall be as rich as you are now poor.'

Truly the man would have had no objection to be rich, but he thought to himself: 'I must first ask my daughter about this,' so he went in and told them that there was a great white bear outside who had faithfully promised to make them all rich if he might but have the youngest daughter.

She said no, and would not hear of it; so the man went out again, and settled with the White Bear that he should come again next Thursday evening, and get her answer. Then the man persuaded her, and talked so much to her about the wealth that they would have, and what a good thing it would be for herself, that at last she made up her mind to go, and washed and mended all her rags, made herself as smart as she could, and held herself in readiness to set out. Little enough had she to take away with her.

Next Thursday evening the White Bear came to fetch her. She seated herself on his back with her bundle, and thus they departed. When they had gone a great part of the way, the White Bear said: 'Are you afraid?'

'No, that I am not,' said she.

'Keep tight hold of my fur, and then there is no danger,' said he.

And thus she rode far, far away, until they came to a great mountain. Then the White Bear knocked on it, and a door opened, and they went into a castle where there were many brilliantly lighted rooms which shone with gold and silver, likewise a large hall in which there was a well-spread table, and it was so magnificent that it would be hard to make anyone understand how splendid it was. The White Bear gave her a silver bell, and told her that when she needed anything she had but to ring this bell, and what she wanted would appear. So after she had eaten, and night was drawing near, she grew sleepy after her journey, and thought she would like to go to bed. She rang the bell, and scarcely had she touched it before she found herself in a chamber where a bed stood ready made for her, which was as pretty as anyone could wish to sleep in. It had pillows of silk, and curtains of silk fringed with gold, and everything that was in the room was of gold or silver, but when she had lain down and put out the light a man came and lay down beside her, and behold it was the White Bear, who cast off the form of a beast during the night. She never saw him, however, for he always came after she had put out her light, and went away before daylight appeared.

So all went well and happily for a time, but then she began to be very sad and sorrowful, for all day long she had to go about alone; and she did so wish to go home to her father and mother and brothers and sisters. Then the White Bear asked what it was that she wanted, and she told him that it was so dull there in the mountain, and that she had to go about all alone, and that in her parents' house at home there were all her brothers and sisters, and it was because she could not go to them that she was so sorrowful.

'There might be a cure for that,' said the White Bear, 'if you would but promise me never to talk with your mother alone, but only when the others are there too; for she will take hold of your hand,' he said, 'and will want to lead you into a room to talk with you alone; but that you must by no means do, or you will bring great misery on both of us.'

So one Sunday the White Bear came and said that they could now set out to see her father and mother, and they journeyed thither, she sitting on his back, and they went a long, long way, and it took a long, long time; but at last they came to a large white farmhouse, and her brothers and sisters were running about outside it, playing, and it was so pretty that it was a pleasure to look at it.

'Your parents dwell here now,' said the White Bear; 'but do not forget what I said to you, or you will do much harm both to yourself and me.'

'No, indeed,' said she, 'I shall never forget;' and as soon as she was at home the White Bear turned round and went back again.

There were such rejoicings when she went in to her parents that it seemed as if they would never come to an end. Everyone thought that he could never be sufficiently grateful to her for all she had done for them all. Now they had everything that they wanted, and everything was as good as it could be. They all asked her how she was getting on where she was. All was well with her too, she said; and she had everything that she could want. What other answers she gave I cannot say, but I am pretty sure that they did not learn much from her. But in the afternoon, after they had dined at midday, all happened just as the White Bear had said. Her mother wanted to talk with her alone in her own chamber. But she remembered what the White Bear had said, and would on no account go. 'What we have to say can be said at any time,' she answered. But somehow or other her mother at last persuaded her, and she was forced to tell the whole story. So she told how every night a man came and lay down beside her when the lights were all put out, and how she never saw him, because he always went away before it grew light in the morning, and how she continually went about in sadness, think-ing how happy she would be if she could but see him, and how all day long she had to go about alone, and it was so dull and solitary. 'Oh!' cried the mother, in horror, 'you are very likely sleeping with a troll! But I will teach you a way to see him. You shall have a bit of one of my candles, which you can take away with you hidden in your breast. Look at him with that when he is asleep, but take care not to let any tallow drop upon him.'

So she took the candle, and hid it in her breast, and when evening drew near the White Bear came to fetch her away. When they had gone some distance on their way, the White Bear asked her if everything had not happened just as he had foretold, and she could not but own that it had. 'Then, if you have done what your mother wished,' said he, 'you have brought great misery on both of us.' 'No,' she said, 'I have not done anything at all.' So when she had reached home and had gone to bed it was just the same as it had been before, and a man came and lay down beside her, and late at night, when she could hear that he was sleeping, she got up and kindled a light, lit her candle, let her light shine on him, and saw him, and he was the handsomest prince that eyes had ever beheld, and she loved him so much that it seemed to her that she must die if she did not kiss him that very moment. So she did kiss him; but while she was doing it she let three drops of hot tallow fall upon his shirt, and he awoke. 'What have you done now?' said he; 'you have brought misery on both of us. If you had but held out for the space of one year I should have been free. I have a stepmother who has bewitched me so that I am a white bear by day and a man by night; but now all is at an end between you and me, and I must leave you, and go to her. She lives in a castle which lies east of the sun and west of the moon, and there too is a princess with a nose which is three ells long, and she now is the one whom I must marry.'

She wept and lamented, but all in vain, for go he must. Then she asked him if she could not go with him. But no, that could not be. 'Can you tell me the way then, and I will seek you – that I may surely be allowed to do!'

'Yes, you may do that,' said he; 'but there is no way thither. It lies east of the sun and west of the moon, and never would you find your way there.'

When she awoke in the morning both the Prince and the castle were gone, and she was lying on a small green patch in the midst of a dark, thick wood. By her side lay the self-same bundle of rags which she had brought with her from her own home. So when she had rubbed the sleep out of her eyes, and wept till she was weary, she set out on her way, and thus she walked for many and many a long day, until at last she came to a great mountain. Outside it an aged woman was sitting, playing with a golden apple. The girl asked her if she knew the way to the Prince who lived with his stepmother in the castle which lay east of the sun and west of the moon, and who was to marry a princess with a nose which was three ells long. 'How do you happen to know about him?' inquired the old woman; 'maybe you are she who ought to have had him.' 'Yes, indeed, I am,' she said. 'So it is you, then?' said the old woman; 'I know nothing about him but that he dwells in a castle which is east of the sun and west of the moon. You will be a long time in getting to it, if ever you get to it at all; but you shall have the loan of my horse, and then you can ride on it to an old woman who is a neighbour of mine: perhaps she can tell you about him. When you have got there you must just strike the horse beneath the left ear and bid it go home again; but you may take the golden apple with you.'

So the girl seated herself on the horse, and rode for a long, long way, and at last she came to the mountain, where an aged woman was sitting outside with a gold carding-comb. The girl asked her if she knew the way to the castle which lay east of the sun and west of the moon; but she said what the first old woman had said: 'I know nothing about it, but that it is east of the sun and west of the moon, and that you will be a long time in getting to it, if ever you get there at all; but you shall have the loan of my horse to an old woman who lives the nearest to me: perhaps she may know where the castle is, and when you have got to her you may just strike the horse beneath the left ear and bid it go home again.' Then she gave her the gold carding-comb, for it might, perhaps, be of use to her, she said.

So the girl seated herself on the horse, and rode a wearisome long way onward again, and after a very long time she came to a great mountain, where an aged woman was sitting, spinning at a golden spinning-wheel. Of this woman, too, she inquired if she knew the way to the Prince, and where to find the castle which lay east of the sun and west of the moon. But it was only the same thing once again. 'Maybe it was you who should have had the Prince,' said the old woman. 'Yes, indeed, I should have been the one,' said the girl. But this old crone knew the way no better than the others – it was east of the sun and west of the moon, she knew that, 'and you will be a long time in getting to it, if ever you get to it at all,' she said; 'but you may have the loan of my horse, and I think you had better ride to the East Wind, and ask him: perhaps he may know where the castle is, and will blow you thither. But when you have got to him you must just strike the horse beneath the left ear, and he will come home again.' And then she gave her the golden spinning-wheel, saying: 'Perhaps you may find that you have a use for it.'

The girl had to ride for a great many days, and for a long and wearisome time, before she got there; but at last she did arrive, and then she asked the East Wind if he could tell her the way to the Prince who dwelt east of the sun and west of the moon. 'Well,' said the East Wind, 'I have heard tell of the Prince, and of his castle, but I do not know the way to it, for I have never blown so far; but, if you like, I will go with you to my brother the West Wind: he may know that, for he is much stronger than I am. You may sit on my back, and then I can carry you there.' So she seated herself on his back, and they did go so swiftly! When they got there, the East Wind went in and said that the girl whom he had brought was the one who ought to have had the Prince up at the castle which lay east of the sun and west of the moon, and that now she was travelling about to find him again, so he had come there with her, and would like to hear if the West Wind knew whereabout the castle was. 'No,' said the West Wind; 'so far as that have I never blown; but if you like I will go with you to the South Wind, for he is much stronger than either of us, and he has roamed far and wide, and perhaps he can tell you what you want to know. You may seat your-self on my back, and then I will carry you to him.'

So she did this, and journeyed to the South Wind, neither was she very long on the way. When they had got there, the West Wind asked him if he could tell her the way to the castle that lay east of the sun and west of the moon, for she was the girl who ought to marry the Prince who lived there. 'Oh, indeed!' said the South Wind, 'is that she? Well,' said he, 'I have wandered about a great deal in my time, and in all kinds of places, but I have never blown so far as that. If you like, however, I will go with you to my brother, the North Wind; he is the oldest and strongest of all of us, and if he does not know where it is no one in the whole world will be able to tell you. You may sit upon my back, and then I will carry you there.' So she seated herself on his back, and off he went from his house in great haste, and they were not long on the way. When they came near the North Wind's dwelling, he was so wild and frantic that they felt cold gusts a long while before they got there. 'What do you want?' he roared out from afar, and they froze as they heard. Said the South Wind: 'It is I, and this is she who should have had the Prince who lives in the castle which lies east of the sun and west of the moon. And now she wishes to ask you if you have ever been there, and can tell her the way, for she would gladly find him again.'

'Yes,' said the North Wind, 'I know where it is. I once blew an aspen leaf there, but I was so tired that for many days afterward I was not able to blow at all. However, if you really are anxious to go there, and are not afraid to go with me, I will take you on my back, and try if I can blow you there.'

'Get there I must,' said she; 'and if there is any way of going I will; and I have no fear, no matter how fast you go.'

'Very well then,' said the North Wind; 'but you must sleep here to-night, for if we are ever to get there we must have the day before us.'

The North Wind woke her betimes next morning, and puffed himself up, and made himself so big and so strong that it was frightful to see him, and away they went, high up through the air, as if they would not stop until they had reached the very end of the world. Down below there was such a storm! It blew down woods and houses, and when they were above the sea the ships were wrecked by hundreds. And thus they tore on and on, and a long time went by, and then yet more time passed, and still they were above the sea, and the North Wind grew tired, and more tired, and at last so utterly weary that he was scarcely able to blow any longer, and he sank and sank, lower and lower, until at last he went so low that the waves dashed against the heels of the poor girl he was carrying. 'Art thou afraid?' said the North Wind. 'I have no fear,' said she; and it was true. But they were not very, very far from land, and there was just enough strength left in the North Wind to enable him to throw her on to the shore, immediately under the windows of a castle which lay east of the sun and west of the moon; but then he was so weary and worn out that he was forced to rest for several days before he could go to his own home again.

Next morning she sat down beneath the walls of the castle to play with the golden apple, and the first person she saw was the maiden with the long nose, who was to have the Prince. 'How much do you want for that gold apple of yours, girl?' said she, opening the window. 'It can't be bought either for gold or money,' answered the girl. 'If it cannot be bought either for gold or money, what will buy it? You may say what you please,' said the Princess.

'Well, if I may go to the Prince who is here, and be with him to-night, you shall have it,' said the girl who had come with the North Wind. 'You may do that,' said the Princess, for she had made up her mind what she would do. So the Princess got the golden apple, but when the girl went up to the Prince's apartment that night he was asleep, for the Princess had so contrived it. The poor girl called to him, and shook him, and between whiles she wept; but she could not wake him. In the morning, as soon as day dawned, in came the Princess with the long nose, and drove her out again. In the daytime she sat down once more beneath the windows of the castle, and began to card with her golden carding-comb; and then all happened as it had happened before. The Princess asked her what she wanted for it, and she replied that it was not for sale, either for gold or money, but that if she could get leave to go to the Prince, and be with him during the night, she should have it. But when she went up to the Prince's room he was again asleep, and, let her call him, or shake him, or weep as she would, he still slept on, and she could not put any life in him. When daylight came in the morning, the Princess with the long nose came too, and once more drove her away. When day had quite come, the girl seated herself under the castle windows, to spin with her golden spinning-wheel, and the Princess with the long nose wanted to have that also. So she opened the window, and asked what she would take for it. The girl said what she had said on each of the former occasions

– that it was not for sale either for gold or for money, but if she could get leave to go to the Prince who lived there, and be with him during the night, she should have it.

'Yes,' said the Princess, 'I will gladly consent to that.'

But in that place there were some Christian folk who had been carried off, and they had been sitting in the chamber which was next to that of the Prince, and had heard how a woman had been in there who had wept and called on him two nights running, and they told the Prince of this. So that evening, when the Princess came once more with her sleeping-drink, he pretended to drink, but threw it away behind him, for he suspected that it was a sleeping-drink. So, when the girl went into the Prince's room this time he was awake, and she had to tell him how she had come there. 'You have come just in time,' said the Prince, 'for I should have been married to-morrow; but I will not have the long-nosed Princess, and you alone can save me. I will say that I want to see what my bride can do, and bid her wash the shirt which has the three drops of tallow on it. This she will consent to do, for she does not know that it is you who let them fall on it; but no one can wash them out but one born of Christian folk: it cannot be done by one of a pack of trolls; and then I will say that no one shall ever be my bride but the woman who can do this, and I know that you can.' There was great joy and gladness between them all that night, but the next day, when the wedding was to take place, the Prince said, 'I must see what my bride can do.' 'That you may do,' said the stepmother.

'I have a fine shirt which I want to wear as my wedding shirt, but three drops of tallow have got upon it which I want to have washed off, and I have vowed to marry no one but the woman who is able to do it. If she cannot do that, she is not worth having.'

Well, that was a very small matter, they thought, and agreed to do it. The Princess with the long nose began to wash as well as she could, but, the more she washed and rubbed, the larger the spots grew. 'Ah! you can't wash at all,' said the old troll-hag, who was her mother. 'Give it to me.' But she too had not had the shirt very long in her hands before it looked worse still, and, the more she washed it and rubbed it, the larger and blacker grew the spots.

So the other trolls had to come and wash, but, the more they did, the blacker and uglier grew the shirt, until at length it was as black as if it had been up the chimney. 'Oh,' cried the Prince, 'not one of you is good for anything at all! There is a beggar-girl sitting outside the window, and I'll be bound that she can wash better than any of you! Come in, you girl there!' he cried. So she came in. 'Can you wash this shirt clean?' he cried. 'Oh! I don't know,' she said; 'but I will try.' And no sooner had she taken the shirt and dipped it in the water than it was white as driven snow, and even whiter than that. 'I will marry you,' said the Prince.

Then the old troll-hag flew into such a rage that she burst, and the Princess with the long nose and all the little trolls must have burst too, for they have never been heard of since. The Prince and his bride set free all the Christian folk who were imprisoned there, and took away with them all the gold and silver that they could carry, and moved far away from the castle which lay east of the sun and west of the moon.

Wanderer's Night Song

GOETHE, *trans.* HENRY W. LONGFELLOW

O'er all the hilltops
Is quiet now,
In all the treetops
Hearest thou
Hardly a breath;
The birds are asleep in the trees:
Wait, soon like these
Thou too shalt rest.

The Selfish Giant

OSCAR WILDE

*E*very afternoon, as they were coming from school, the children used to go and play in the Giant's garden.

It was a large lovely garden, with soft green grass. Here and there over the grass stood beautiful flowers like stars, and there were twelve peach-trees that in the springtime broke out into delicate blossoms of pink and pearl, and in the autumn bore rich fruit. The birds sat on the trees and sang so sweetly that the children used to stop their games in order to listen to them. 'How happy we are here!' they cried to each other.

One day the Giant came back. He had been to visit his friend the Cornish ogre, and had stayed with him for seven years. After the seven years were over he had said all that he had to say, for his conversation was limited, and he determined to return to his own castle. When he arrived he saw the children playing in the garden.

'What are you doing here?' he cried in a very gruff voice, and the children ran away.

'My own garden is my own garden,' said the Giant; 'anyone can understand that, and I will allow nobody to play in it but myself.' So he built a high wall all round it, and put up a notice-board.

> TRESPASSERS
> WILL BE
> PROSECUTED

He was a very selfish Giant.

The poor children had now nowhere to play. They tried to play on the road, but the road was very dusty and full of hard stones, and they did not like it. They used to wander round the high wall when their lessons were over, and talk about the beautiful garden inside. 'How happy we were there,' they said to each other.

Then the Spring came, and all over the country there were little blossoms and little birds. Only in the garden of the Selfish Giant it was still winter. The birds did not care to sing in it as there were no children, and the trees forgot to blossom. Once a beautiful flower put its head out from the grass, but when it saw the notice-board it was so sorry for the children that it slipped back into the ground again, and went off to sleep. The only people who were pleased were the Snow and the Frost. 'Spring has forgotten this garden,' they cried, 'so we will live here all the year round.' The Snow covered up the grass with her great white cloak, and the Frost painted all the trees silver. Then they invited the North Wind to stay with them, and he came. He was wrapped in furs, and he roared all day about the garden, and blew the chimney-pots down. 'This is a delightful spot,' he said, 'we must ask the Hail on a visit.' So the Hail came. Every day for three hours he rattled on the roof of the castle till he broke most of the slates, and then he ran round and round the garden as fast as he could go. He was dressed in grey, and his breath was like ice.

'I cannot understand why the Spring is so late in coming,' said the Selfish Giant, as he sat at the window and looked out at his cold white garden; 'I hope there will be a change in the weather.'

But the Spring never came, nor the Summer. The Autumn gave golden fruit to every garden, but to the Giant's garden she gave none. 'He is too selfish,' she said. So it was always winter there, and the North Wind, and the Hail, and the Frost, and the Snow danced about through the trees.

One morning the Giant was lying awake in bed when he heard some lovely music. It sounded so sweet to his ears that he thought it must be the King's musicians passing by. It was really only a little linnet singing outside his window, but it was so long since he had heard a bird sing in his garden that it seemed to him to be the most beautiful music in the world. Then the Hail stopped dancing over his head, and the North Wind ceased roaring, and a delicious perfume came to him through the open casement. 'I believe the Spring has come at last,' said the Giant; and he jumped out of bed and looked out.

What did he see?

He saw a most wonderful sight. Through a little hole in the wall the children had crept in, and they were sitting in the branches of the trees. In every tree that he could see there was a little child. And the trees were so glad to have the children back again that they had covered themselves with blossoms, and were waving their arms gently above the children's heads. The birds were flying about and twittering with delight, and the flowers were looking up through the green grass and laughing. It was a lovely scene, only in one corner it was still winter. It was the farthest corner of the garden, and in it was standing a little boy. He was so small that he could not reach up to the branches of the tree, and he was wandering all round it, crying bitterly. The poor tree was still quite covered with frost and snow, and the North Wind was blowing and roaring above it. 'Climb up! little boy,' said the Tree, and it bent its branches down as low as it could; but the boy was too tiny.

And the Giant's heart melted as he looked out. 'How selfish I have been!' he said; 'now I know why the Spring would not come here. I will put that poor little boy on the top of the tree, and then I will knock down the wall, and my garden shall be the children's playground for ever and ever.' He was really very sorry for what he had done.

So he crept downstairs and opened the front door quite softly, and went out into the garden. But when the children saw him they were so frightened that they all ran away, and the garden became winter again. Only the little boy did not run, for his eyes were so full of tears that he did not see the Giant coming. And the Giant stole up behind him and took him gently in his hand, and put him up into the tree. And the tree broke at once into blossom, and the birds came and sang on it, and the little boy stretched out his two arms and flung them round the Giant's neck, and kissed him. And the other children, when they saw that the Giant was not wicked any longer, came running back, and with them came the Spring. 'It is your garden now, little children,' said the Giant, and he took a great axe and knocked down the wall. And when the people were going to market at twelve o'clock they found the Giant playing with the children in the most beautiful garden they had ever seen.

All day long they played, and in the evening they came to the Giant to bid him good-bye.

'But where is your little companion?' he said: 'the boy I put into the tree.' The Giant loved him the best because he had kissed him.

'We don't know,' answered the children; 'he has gone away.'

'You must tell him to be sure and come here to-morrow,' said the Giant. But the children said that they did not know where he lived, and had never seen him before; and the Giant felt very sad.

Every afternoon, when school was over, the children came and played with the Giant. But the little boy whom the Giant loved was never seen again. The Giant was very kind to all the children, yet he longed for his first little friend, and often spoke of him. 'How I would like to see him!' he used to say.

Years went over, and the Giant grew very old and feeble. He could not play about any more, so he sat in a huge armchair, and watched the children at their games, and admired his garden. 'I have many beautiful flowers,' he said; 'but the children are the most beautiful flowers of all.'

One winter morning he looked out of his window as he was dressing. He did not hate the Winter now, for he knew that it was merely the Spring asleep, and that the flowers were resting.

Suddenly he rubbed his eyes in wonder, and looked and looked. It certainly was a marvellous sight. In the farthest corner of the garden was a tree quite covered with lovely white blossoms. Its branches were all golden, and silver fruit hung down from them, and underneath it stood the little boy he had loved.

Downstairs ran the Giant in great joy, and out into the garden. He hastened across the grass, and came near to the child. And when he came quite close his face grew red with anger, and he said, 'Who hath dared to wound thee?' For on the palms of the child's hands were the prints of two nails, and the prints of two nails were on the little feet.

'Who hath dared to wound thee?' cried the Giant; 'tell me, that I may take my big sword and slay him.'

'Nay!' answered the child; 'but these are the wounds of Love.'

'Who art thou?' said the Giant, and a strange awe fell on him, and he knelt before the little child.

And the child smiled on the Giant, and said to him, 'You let me play once in your garden, to-day you shall come with me to my garden, which is Paradise.'

And when the children ran in that afternoon, they found the Giant lying dead under the tree, all covered with white blossoms.

A Pair of Silk Stockings

KATE CHOPIN

*L*ittle Mrs Sommers one day found herself the unexpected
possessor of fifteen dollars. It seemed to her a very large
amount of money, and the way in which it stuffed and bulged her
worn old *porte-monnaie* gave her a feeling of importance such
as she had not enjoyed for years.

The question of investment was one that occupied her greatly.
For a day or two she walked about apparently in a dreamy state,
but really absorbed in speculation and calculation. She did not
wish to act hastily, to do anything she might afterward regret.
But it was during the still hours of the night when she lay awake
revolving plans in her mind that she seemed to see her way clearly
toward a proper and judicious use of the money.

A dollar or two should be added to the price usually paid for
Janie's shoes, which would insure their lasting an appreciable
time longer than they usually did. She would buy so and so many
yards of percale for new shirt waists for the boys and Janie and
Mag. She had intended to make the old ones do by skilful patch-
ing. Mag should have another gown. She had seen some

beautiful patterns, veritable bargains in the shop windows. And still there would be left enough for new stockings – two pairs apiece – and what darning that would save for a while! She would get caps for the boys and sailor-hats for the girls. The vision of her little brood looking fresh and dainty and new for once in their lives excited her and made her restless and wakeful with anticipation.

The neighbours sometimes talked of certain 'better days' that little Mrs Sommers had known before she had ever thought of being Mrs Sommers. She herself indulged in no such morbid retrospection. She had no time – no second of time to devote to the past. The needs of the present absorbed her every faculty. A vision of the future like some dim, gaunt monster sometimes appalled her, but luckily to-morrow never comes.

Mrs Sommers was one who knew the value of bargains; who could stand for hours making her way inch by inch toward the desired object that was selling below cost. She could elbow her way if need be; she had learned to clutch a piece of goods and hold it and stick to it with persistence and determination till her turn came to be served, no matter when it came.

But that day she was a little faint and tired. She had swallowed a light luncheon – no! when she came to think of it, between getting the children fed and the place righted, and preparing herself for the shopping bout, she had actually forgotten to eat any luncheon at all!

She sat herself upon a revolving stool before a counter that was comparatively deserted, trying to gather strength and cour-age to charge through an eager multitude that was besieging breast-works of shirting and figured lawn. An all-gone limp feeling had come over her and she rested her hand aimlessly upon the counter. She wore no gloves. By degrees she grew aware that her hand had encountered something very soothing, very pleasant to touch. She looked down to see that her hand lay upon a pile of silk stockings. A placard near by announced that they had been reduced in price from two dollars and fifty cents to one dollar and ninety-eight cents; and a young girl who stood behind the counter asked her if she wished to examine their line of silk hosiery. She smiled, just as if she had been asked to inspect a tiara of diamonds with the ultimate view of purchasing it. But she went on feeling the soft, sheeny luxurious things – with both hands now, holding them up to see them glisten, and to feel them glide serpent-like through her fingers.

Two hectic blotches came suddenly into her pale cheeks. She looked up at the girl.

'Do you think there are any eights-and-a-half among these?'

There were any number of eights-and-a-half. In fact, there were more of that size than any other. Here was a light-blue pair; there were some lavender, some all black and various shades of tan and grey. Mrs Sommers selected a black pair and looked at them very long and closely. She pretended to be examining their texture, which the clerk assured her was excellent.

'A dollar and ninety-eight cents,' she mused aloud. 'Well, I'll take this pair.' She handed the girl a five-dollar bill and waited for her change and for her parcel. What a very small parcel it was. It seemed lost in the depths of her shabby old shopping-bag.

Mrs Sommers after that did not move in the direction of the bargain counter. She took the elevator, which carried her to an upper floor into the region of the ladies' waiting-rooms. Here, in a retired corner, she exchanged her cotton stockings for the new silk ones which she had just bought. She was not going through any acute mental process or reasoning with herself, nor was she striving to explain to her satisfaction the motive of her action. She was not thinking at all. She seemed for the time to be taking a rest from that laborious and fatiguing function and to have abandoned herself to some mechanical impulse that directed her actions and freed her of responsibility.

How good was the touch of the raw silk to her flesh! She felt like lying back in the cushioned chair and revelling for a while in the luxury of it. She did for a little while. Then she replaced her shoes, rolled the cotton stockings together and thrust them into her bag. After doing this she crossed straight over to the shoe department and took her seat to be fitted.

She was fastidious. The clerk could not make her out; he could not reconcile her shoes with her stockings, and she was not too easily pleased. She held back her skirts and turned her feet one way and her head another way as she glanced down at the polished, pointed-tipped boots. Her foot and ankle looked very pretty. She could not realise that they belonged to her and were a part of herself. She wanted an excellent and stylish fit, she told the young fellow who served her, and she did not mind the difference of a dollar or two more in the price so long as she got what she desired.

It was a long time since Mrs Sommers had been fitted with gloves. On rare occasions when she had bought a pair they were always 'bargains', so cheap that it would have been preposterous and unreasonable to have expected them to be fitted to the hand.

Now she rested her elbow on the cushion of the glove counter, and a pretty, pleasant young creature, delicate and deft of touch, drew a long-wristed 'kid' over Mrs Sommers' hand. She smoothed it down over the wrist and buttoned it neatly, and both lost themselves for a second or two in admiring contemplation of the little symmetrical gloved hand. But there were other places where money might be spent.

There were books and magazines piled up in the window of a stall a few paces down the street. Mrs Sommers bought two high-priced magazines such as she had been accustomed to read in the days when she had been accustomed to other pleasant things. She carried them without wrapping. As well as she could she lifted her skirts at the crossings. Her stockings and boots and well-fitting gloves had worked marvels in her bearing – had given her a feeling of assurance, a sense of belonging to the well-dressed multitude.

She was very hungry. Another time she would have stifled the cravings for food until reaching her own home, where she would have brewed herself a cup of tea and taken a snack of anything that was available. But the impulse that was guiding her would not suffer her to entertain any such thought.

There was a restaurant at the corner. She had never entered its doors; from the outside she had sometimes caught glimpses of spotless damask and shining crystal, and soft-stepping waiters serving people of fashion.

When she entered her appearance created no surprise, no consternation, as she had half feared it might. She seated herself at a small table alone, and an attentive waiter at once approached to take her order. She did not want a profusion; she craved a nice and tasty bite – a half-dozen blue points, a plump chop with cress, a something sweet – crème-frappée, for instance; a glass of Rhine wine, and after all a small cup of black coffee.

While waiting to be served she removed her gloves very leisurely and laid them beside her. Then she picked up a magazine and glanced through it, cutting the pages with a blunt edge of her knife. It was all very agreeable. The damask was even more spotless than it had seemed through the window, and the crystal more sparkling. There were quiet ladies and gentlemen, who did not notice her, lunching at the small tables like her own. A soft, pleasing strain of music could be heard, and a gentle breeze was blowing through the window. She tasted a bite, and she read a word or two, and she sipped the amber wine and wiggled her toes in the silk stockings. The price of it made no difference. She counted the money out to the waiter and left an extra coin on his tray, whereupon he bowed before her as before a princess of royal blood.

There was still money in her purse, and her next temptation presented itself in the shape of a matinée poster.

It was a little later when she entered the theatre, the play had begun and the house seemed to her to be packed. But there were vacant seats here and there, and into one of them she was ushered, between brilliantly dressed women who had gone there to kill time and eat candy and display their gaudy attire. There were many others who were there solely for the play and acting. It is safe to say there was no one present who bore quite the attitude which Mrs Sommers did to her surroundings. She gathered in the whole – stage and players and people in one wide impression, and absorbed it and enjoyed it. She laughed at the comedy and wept – she and the gaudy woman next to her wept over the tragedy. And they talked a little together over it. And the gaudy woman wiped her eyes and sniffed on a tiny square of filmy, perfumed lace and passed little Mrs Sommers her box of candy.

The play was over, the music ceased, the crowd filed out. It was like a dream ended. People scattered in all directions. Mrs Sommers went to the corner and waited for the cable car.

A man with keen eyes, who sat opposite to her, seemed to like the study of her small, pale face. It puzzled him to decipher what he saw there. In truth he saw nothing – unless he were wizard enough to detect a poignant wish, a powerful longing that the cable car would never stop anywhere, but go on and on with her for ever.

The Aunt and Amabel

E. NESBIT

*I*t is not pleasant to be a fish out of water. To be a cat in water is not what anyone would desire. To be in a temper is uncomfortable. And no one can fully taste the joys of life if he is in a Little Lord Fauntleroy suit. But by far the most uncomfortable thing to be in is disgrace, sometimes amusingly called Coventry by the people who are not in it.

We have all been there. It is a place where the heart sinks and aches, where familiar faces are clouded and changed, where any remark that one may tremblingly make is received with stony silence or with the assurance that nobody wants to talk to such a naughty child. If you are only in disgrace, and not in solitary confinement, you will creep about a house that is like the one you have had such jolly times in, and yet as unlike it as a bad dream is to a June morning. You will long to speak to people, and be afraid to speak. You will wonder whether there is anything you can do that will change things at all. You have said you are sorry, and that has changed nothing. You will wonder whether you are to stay for ever in this desolate place, outside all hope and love and fun and happiness. And though it has happened before, and has always, in the end, come to an end, you can never be quite sure that this time it is not going to last for ever.

'It *is* going to last for ever,' said Amabel, who was eight. 'What shall I do? Oh whatever shall I do?'

What she *had* done ought to have formed the subject of her meditations. And she had done what had seemed to her all the time, and in fact still seemed, a self-sacrificing and noble act. She was staying with an aunt – measles or a new baby, or the painters in the house, I forget which, the cause of her banishment. And the aunt, who was really a great-aunt and quite old enough to know better, had been grumbling about her head gardener to a lady who called in blue spectacles and a beady bonnet with violet flowers in it.

'He hardly lets me have a plant for the table,' said the aunt, 'and that border in front of the breakfast-room window – it's just bare earth – and I expressly ordered chrysanthemums to be planted there. He thinks of nothing but his greenhouse.'

The beady-violet-blue-glassed lady snorted, and said she didn't know what we were coming to, and she would have just half a cup, please, with not quite so much milk, thank you very much.

Now what would you have done? Minded your own business most likely, and not got into trouble at all. Not so Amabel. Enthusiastically anxious to do something which should make the great-aunt see what a thoughtful, unselfish, little girl she really was (the aunt's opinion of her being at present quite other-wise), she got up very early in the morning and took the cutting-out scissors from the work-room table drawer and stole, 'like an errand of mercy,' she told herself, to the greenhouse where she busily snipped off every single flower she could find. MacFarlane was at his breakfast. Then with the points of the cutting-out scissors she made nice deep little holes in the flower-bed where the chrysanthemums ought to have been, and struck the flowers in – chrysanthemums, geraniums, primulas, orchids, and carnations. It would be a lovely surprise for Auntie.

Then the aunt came down to breakfast and saw the lovely surprise. Amabel's world turned upside down and inside out suddenly and surprisingly, and there she was, in Coventry, and not even the housemaid would speak to her. Her great-uncle, whom she passed in the hall on her way to her own room, did indeed, as he smoothed his hat, murmur, 'Sent to Coventry, eh? Never mind, it'll soon be over,' and went off to the City banging the front door behind him.

He meant well, but he did not understand.

Amabel understood, or she thought she did, and knew in her miserable heart that she was sent to Coventry for the last time, and that this time she would stay there.

'I don't care,' she said quite untruly. 'I'll never try to be kind to anyone again.' And that wasn't true either. She was to spend the whole day alone in the best bedroom, the one with the four-post bed and the red curtains and the large wardrobe with a looking-glass in it that you could see yourself in to the very ends of your strap-shoes.

The first thing Amabel did was to look at herself in the glass. She was still sniffing and sobbing, and her eyes were swimming in tears, another one rolled down her nose as she looked – that was very interesting. Another rolled down, and that was the last, because as soon as you get interested in watching your tears they stop.

Next she looked out of the window, and saw the decorated flower-bed, just as she had left it, very bright and beautiful.

'Well, it *does* look nice,' she said. 'I don't care what they say.'

Then she looked round the room for something to read; there was nothing. The old-fashioned best bedrooms never did have anything. Only on the large dressing-table, on the left-hand side of the oval swing-glass, was one book covered in red velvet, and on it, very twistily embroidered in yellow silk and mixed up with misleading leaves and squiggles were the letters, A.B.C.

'Perhaps it's a picture alphabet,' said Mabel, and was quite pleased, though of course she was much too old to care for alphabets. Only when one is very unhappy and very dull, anything is better than nothing. She opened the book.

'Why, it's only a time-table!' she said. 'I suppose it's for people when they want to go away, and Auntie puts it here in case they suddenly make up their minds to go, and feel that they can't wait another minute. I feel like that, only it's no good, and I expect other people do too.'

She had learned how to use the dictionary, and this seemed to go the same way. She looked up the names of all the places she knew – Brighton where she had once spent a month, Rugby where her brother was at school, and Home, which was Amberley – and she saw the times when the trains left for these places, and wished she could go by those trains.

And once more she looked round the best bedroom which was her prison, and thought of the Bastille, and wished she had a toad to tame, like the poor Viscount, or a flower to watch growing, like Picciola, and she was very sorry for herself, and very angry with her aunt, and very grieved at the conduct of her parents – she had expected better things from them – and now they had left her in this dreadful place where no one loved her, and no one understood her.

There seemed to be no place for toads or flowers in the best room, it was carpeted all over even in its least noticeable corners. It had everything a best room ought to have – and everything was of dark shining mahogany. The toilet-table had a set of red and gold glass things – a tray, candlesticks, a ring-stand, many little pots with lids, and two bottles with stoppers. When the stoppers were taken out they smelt very strange, something like very old scent, and something like cold cream also very old, and something like going to the dentist's.

I do not know whether the scent of those bottles had anything to do with what happened. It certainly was a very extraordinary scent. Quite different from any perfume that I smell nowadays, but I remember that when I was a little girl I smelt it quite often. But then there are no best rooms now such as there used to be. The best rooms now are gay with chintz and mirrors, and there are always flowers and books, and little tables to put your teacup on, and sofas, and armchairs. And they smell of varnish and new furniture.

When Amabel had sniffed at both bottles and looked in all the pots, which were quite clean and empty except for a pearl button and two pins in one of them, she took up the A.B.C. again to look for Whitby, where her godmother lived. And it was then that she saw the extraordinary name '*Whereyouwantogoto*'. This was odd – but the name of the station from which it started was still more extraordinary, for it was not Euston or Cannon Street or Marylebone.

The name of the station was '*Bigwardrobeinspareroom*'. And below this name, really quite unusual for a station, Amabel read in small letters:

'Single fares strictly forbidden. Return tickets No Class Nuppence. Trains leave *Bigwardrobeinspareroom* all the time.'

And under that in still smaller letters –

'*You had better go now.*'

What would you have done? Rubbed your eyes and thought you were dreaming? Well, if you had, nothing more would have happened. Nothing ever does when you behave like that. Amabel was wiser. She went straight to the Big Wardrobe and turned its glass handle.

'I expect it's only shelves and people's best hats,' she said. But she only said it. People often say what they don't mean, so that if things turn out as they don't expect, they can say 'I told you so,' but this is most dishonest to one's self, and being dishonest to one's self is almost worse than being dishonest to other people. Amabel would never have done it if she had been herself. But she was out of herself with anger and unhappiness.

Of course it wasn't hats. It was, most amazingly, a crystal cave, very oddly shaped like a railway station. It seemed to be lighted by stars, which is, of course, unusual in a booking office, and over the station clock was a full moon. The clock had no figures, only *Now* in shining letters all round it, twelve times, and the *Nows* touched, so the clock was bound to be always right. How different from the clock you go to school by!

A porter in white satin hurried forward to take Amabel's luggage. Her luggage was the A.B.C. which she still held in her hand.

'Lots of time, Miss,' he said, grinning in a most friendly way, 'I *am* glad you're going. You *will* enjoy yourself! What a nice little girl you are!'

This was cheering. Amabel smiled.

At the pigeon-hole that tickets come out of, another person, also in white satin, was ready with a mother-of-pearl ticket, round, like a card counter.

'Here you are, Miss,' he said with the kindest smile, 'price nothing, and refreshments free all the way. It's a pleasure,' he added, 'to issue a ticket to a nice little lady like you.' The train was entirely of crystal, too, and the cushions were of white satin. There were little buttons such as you have for electric bells, and on them 'Whatyouwantoeat', 'Whatyouwantodrink', 'Whatyouwantoread', in silver letters.

Amabel pressed all the buttons at once, and instantly felt obliged to blink. The blink over, she saw on the cushion by her side a silver tray with vanilla ice, boiled chicken and white sauce, almonds (blanched), peppermint creams, and mashed potatoes, and a long glass of lemonade – beside the tray was a book. It was Mrs Ewing's *Bad-tempered Family*, and it was bound in white vellum.

There is nothing more luxurious than eating while you read – unless it be reading while you eat. Amabel did both: they are not the same thing, as you will see if you think the matter over.

And just as the last thrill of the last spoonful of ice died away, and the last full stop of the *Bad-tempered Family* met Amabel's eye, the train stopped, and hundreds of railway officials in white velvet shouted, '*Whereyouwantogoto!* Get out!'

A velvety porter, who was somehow like a silkworm as well as like a wedding handkerchief sachet, opened the door.

'Now!' he said, 'come on out, Miss Amabel, unless you want to go to *Whereyoudon'twantogoto.*'

She hurried out, on to an ivory platform.

'Not on the ivory, if you please,' said the porter, 'the white Axminster carpet – it's laid down expressly for you.'

Amabel walked along it and saw ahead of her a crowd, all in white.

'What's all that?' she asked the friendly porter.

'It's the Mayor, dear Miss Amabel,' he said, 'with your address.'

'My address is The Old Cottage, Amberley,' she said, 'at least it used to be' – and found herself face to face with the Mayor. He was very like Uncle George, but he bowed low to her, which was not Uncle George's habit, and said:

'Welcome, dear little Amabel. Please accept this admiring address from the Mayor and burgesses and apprentices and all the rest of it, of Whereyouwantogoto.'

The address was in silver letters, on white silk, and it said:

'Welcome, dear Amabel. We know you meant to please your aunt. It was very clever of you to think of putting the greenhouse flowers in the bare flower-bed. You couldn't be expected to know that you ought to ask leave before you touch other people's things.'

'Oh, but,' said Amabel quite confused. 'I did . . .'

But the band struck up, and drowned her words. The instruments of the band were all of silver, and the bandsmen's clothes of white leather. The tune they played was 'Cheero!'

Then Amabel found that she was taking part in a procession, hand in hand with the Mayor, and the band playing like mad all the time. The Mayor was dressed entirely in cloth of silver, and as they went along he kept saying, close to her ear,

'You have our sympathy, you have our sympathy,' till she felt quite giddy.

There was a flower show – all the flowers were white. There was a concert – all the tunes were old ones. There was a play called *Put yourself in her place*. And there was a banquet, with Amabel in the place of honour.

They drank her health in white wine whey, and then through the Crystal Hall of a thousand gleaming pillars, where thousands of guests, all in white, were met to do honour to Amabel, the shout went up – 'Speech, speech!'

I cannot explain to you what had been going on in Amabel's mind. Perhaps you know. Whatever it was it began like a very tiny butterfly in a box, that could not keep quiet, but fluttered, and fluttered, and fluttered. And when the Mayor rose and said:

'Dear Amabel, you whom we all love and understand; dear Amabel, you who were so unjustly punished for trying to give pleasure to an unresponsive aunt; poor, ill-used, ill-treated, innocent Amabel; blameless, suffering Amabel, we await your words,' that fluttering, tiresome butterfly-thing inside her seemed suddenly to swell to the size and strength of a fluttering albatross, and Amabel got up from her seat of honour on the throne of ivory and silver and pearl, and said, choking a little, and extremely red about the ears –

'Ladies and gentlemen, I don't want to make a speech, I just want to say, "Thank you," and to say – to say – to say . . .'

She stopped, and all the white crowd cheered.

'To say,' she went on as the cheers died down, 'that I wasn't blameless, and innocent, and all those nice things. I ought to have thought. And they *were* Auntie's flowers. But I did want to please her. It's all so mixed. Oh, I wish Auntie was here!'

And instantly Auntie *was* there, very tall and quite nice-looking, in a white velvet dress and an ermine cloak.

'Speech,' cried the crowd. 'Speech from Auntie!'

Auntie stood on the step of the throne beside Amabel, and said:

'I think, perhaps, I was hasty. And I think Amabel meant to please me. But all the flowers that were meant for the winter . . . well – I was annoyed. I'm sorry.'

'Oh, Auntie, so am I – so am I,' cried Amabel, and the two began to hug each other on the ivory step, while the crowd cheered like mad, and the band struck up that well-known air, 'If you only understood!'

'Oh, Auntie,' said Amabel among hugs, 'this is such a lovely place, come and see everything, we may, mayn't we?' she asked the Mayor.

'The place is yours,' he said, 'and now you can see many things that you couldn't see before. We are The People who Understand. And now you are one of Us. And your aunt is another.'

I must not tell you all that they saw because these things are secrets only known to The People who Understand, and perhaps you do not yet belong to that happy nation. And if you do, you will know without my telling you.

And when it grew late, and the stars were drawn down, somehow, to hang among the trees, Amabel fell asleep in her aunt's arms beside a white foaming fountain on a marble terrace, where white peacocks came to drink.

She awoke on the big bed in the spare room, but her aunt's arms were still round her.

'Amabel,' she was saying, 'Amabel!'

'Oh, Auntie,' said Amabel sleepily, 'I am so sorry. It *was* stupid of me. And I did mean to please you.'

'It *was* stupid of you,' said the aunt, 'but I am sure you meant to please me. Come down to supper.' And Amabel has a confused recollection of her aunt's saying that she was sorry, adding, 'Poor little Amabel.'

If the aunt really did say it, it was fine of her. And Amabel is quite sure that she did say it.

Amabel and her great-aunt are now the best of friends. But neither of them has ever spoken to the other of the beautiful city called '*Whereyouwantogoto*'. Amabel is too shy to be the first to mention it, and no doubt the aunt has her own reasons for not broaching the subject.

But of course they both know that they have been there together, and it is easy to get on with people when you and they alike belong to the *Peoplewhounderstand*.

If you look in the A.B.C. that your people have you will not find '*Whereyouwantogoto*'. It is only in the red velvet bound copy that Amabel found in her aunt's best bedroom.

Moon Song

MILDRED PLEW MEIGS

Zoon, zoon, cuddle and croon –
    Over the crinkling sea,
The moon man flings him a silvered net
    Fashioned of moonbeams three.

And some folk say when the net lies long
    And the midnight hour is ripe;
The moon man fishes for some old song
    That fell from a sailor's pipe.

And some folk say that he fishes the bars
    Down where the dead ships lie,
Looking for lost little baby stars
    That slid from the slippery sky.

And the waves roll out and the waves roll in
  And the nodding night wind blows,
But why the moon man fishes the sea
  Only the moon man knows.

Zoon, zoon, net of the moon
  Rides on the wrinkling sea;
Bright is the fret and shining wet,
  Fashioned of moonbeams three.

And some folk say when the great net gleams
  And the waves are dusky blue,
The moon man fishes for two little dreams
  He lost when the world was new.

And some folk say in the late night hours,
  While the long fin-shadows slide,
The moon man fishes for cold sea flowers
  Under the tumbling tide.

And the waves roll out and the waves roll in
  And the grey gulls dip and doze,
But why the moon man fishes the sea
  Only the moon man knows.

Zoon, zoon, cuddle and croon –
   Over the crinkling sea,
The moon man flings him a silvered net
   Fashioned of moonbeams three.

And some folk say that he follows the flecks
   Down where the last light flows,
Fishing for two round gold-rimmed 'specs'
   That blew from his button-like nose.

And some folk say while the salt sea foams
   And the silver net lines snare,
The moon man fishes for carven combs
   That float from the mermaids' hair.

And the waves roll out and the waves roll in
   And the nodding night wind blows,
But why the moon man fishes the sea
   Only the moon man knows.

The Wind in the Willows *(excerpt)*

KENNETH GRAHAME

CHAPTER I

The River Bank

The Mole had been working very hard all the morning, spring-cleaning his little home. First with brooms, then with dusters; then on ladders and steps and chairs, with a brush and a pail of whitewash; till he had dust in his throat and eyes, and splashes of whitewash all over his black fur, and an aching back and weary arms. Spring was moving in the air above and in the earth below and around him, penetrating even his dark and lowly little house with its spirit of divine discontent and longing. It was small wonder, then, that he suddenly flung down his brush on the floor, said 'Bother!' and 'O blow!' and also 'Hang spring-cleaning!' and bolted out of the house without even waiting to put on his coat. Something up above was calling him imperiously, and he made for the steep little tunnel which answered in his case to the gravelled carriage-drive owned by animals whose residences are nearer to the sun and air. So he scraped and scratched and scrabbled and scrooged and then he scrooged again and scrabbled and scratched and scraped, working busily with his little paws and muttering to himself, 'Up we go! Up we go!' till at last, pop! his snout came out into the sunlight, and he found himself rolling in the warm grass of a great meadow.

'This is fine!' he said to himself. 'This is better than white-washing!' The sunshine struck hot on his fur, soft breezes caressed his heated brow, and after the seclusion of the cellarage he had lived in so long the carol of happy birds fell on his dulled hearing almost like a shout. Jumping off all his four legs at once, in the joy of living and the delight of spring without its cleaning, he pursued his way across the meadow till he reached the hedge on the further side.

'Hold up!' said an elderly rabbit at the gap. 'Sixpence for the privilege of passing by the private road!' He was bowled over in an instant by the impatient and contemptuous Mole, who trot-ted along the side of the hedge chaffing the other rabbits as they peeped hurriedly from their holes to see what the row was about. 'Onion-sauce! Onion-sauce!' he remarked jeeringly, and was gone before they could think of a thoroughly satisfactory reply. Then they all started grumbling at each other. 'How *stupid* you are! Why didn't you tell him—' 'Well, why didn't *you* say—' 'You might have reminded him—' and so on, in the usual way; but, of course, it was then much too late, as is always the case.

It all seemed too good to be true. Hither and thither through the meadows he rambled busily, along the hedgerows, across the copses, finding everywhere birds building, flowers budding, leaves thrusting – everything happy, and progressive, and

64

occupied. And instead of having an uneasy conscience pricking him and whispering 'Whitewash!' he somehow could only feel how jolly it was to be the only idle dog among all these busy citizens. After all, the best part of a holiday is perhaps not so much to be resting yourself, as to see all the other fellows busy working.

He thought his happiness was complete when, as he meandered aimlessly along, suddenly he stood by the edge of a full-fed river. Never in his life had he seen a river before – this sleek, sinuous, full-bodied animal, chasing and chuckling, gripping things with a gurgle and leaving them with a laugh, to fling itself on fresh playmates that shook themselves free, and were caught and held again. All was a-shake and a-shiver – glints and gleams and sparkles, rustle and swirl, chatter and bubble. The Mole was bewitched, entranced, fascinated. By the side of the river he trotted as one trots, when very small, by the side of a man who holds one spell-bound by exciting stories; and when tired at last, he sat on the bank, while the river still chattered on to him, a babbling procession of the best stories in the world, sent from the heart of the earth to be told at last to the insatiable sea.

As he sat on the grass and looked across the river, a dark hole in the bank opposite, just above the water's edge, caught his eye, and dreamily he fell to considering what a nice snug dwelling-place it would make for an animal with few wants and fond of a bijou riverside residence, above flood level and remote from noise and dust. As he gazed, something bright and small seemed to twinkle down in the heart of it, vanished, then twinkled once more like a tiny star. But it could hardly be a star in such an unlikely situation; and it was too glittering and small for a glow-worm. Then, as he looked, it winked at him, and so declared itself to be an eye; and a small face began gradually to grow up round it, like a frame round a picture.

A brown little face, with whiskers.

A grave round face, with the same twinkle in its eye that had first attracted his notice.

Small neat ears and thick silky hair.

It was the Water Rat!

Then the two animals stood and regarded each other cautiously.

'Hullo, Mole!' said the Water Rat.

'Hullo, Rat!' said the Mole.

'Would you like to come over?' enquired the Rat presently.

'Oh, its all very well to *talk*,' said the Mole, rather pettishly, he being new to a river and riverside life and its ways.

The Rat said nothing, but stooped and unfastened a rope and hauled on it; then lightly stepped into a little boat which the Mole had not observed. It was painted blue outside and white within, and was just the size for two animals; and the Mole's whole heart went out to it at once, even though he did not yet fully understand its uses.

The Rat sculled smartly across and made fast. Then he held up his forepaw as the Mole stepped gingerly down. 'Lean on that!' he said. 'Now then, step lively!' and the Mole to his surprise and rapture found himself actually seated in the stern of a real boat.

'This has been a wonderful day!' said he, as the Rat shoved off and took to the sculls again. 'Do you know, I've never been in a boat before in all my life.'

'What?' cried the Rat, open-mouthed: 'Never been in a – you never – well I – what have you been doing, then?'

'Is it so nice as all that?' asked the Mole shyly, though he was quite prepared to believe it as he leant back in his seat and surveyed the cushions, the oars, the rowlocks, and all the fascinating fittings, and felt the boat sway lightly under him.

'Nice? It's the *only* thing,' said the Water Rat solemnly, as he leant forward for his stroke. 'Believe me, my young friend, there is *nothing* – absolutely nothing – half so much worth doing as simply messing about in boats. Simply messing,' he went on dreamily: 'messing – about – in – boats; messing—'

'Look ahead, Rat!' cried the Mole suddenly.

It was too late. The boat struck the bank full tilt. The dreamer, the joyous oarsman, lay on his back at the bottom of the boat, his heels in the air.

'—about in boats – or *with* boats,' the Rat went on composedly, picking himself up with a pleasant laugh. 'In or out of 'em, it doesn't matter. Nothing seems really to matter, that's the charm of it. Whether you get away, or whether you don't; whether you arrive at your destination or whether you reach somewhere else, or whether you never get anywhere at all, you're always busy, and you never do anything in particular; and when you've done it there's always something else to do, and you can do it if you like, but you'd much better not. Look here! If you've really nothing else on hand this morning, supposing we drop down the river together, and have a long day of it?'

The Mole waggled his toes from sheer happiness, spread his chest with a sigh of full contentment, and leaned back blissfully into the soft cushions. '*What* a day I'm having!' he said. 'Let us start at once!'

'Hold hard a minute, then!' said the Rat. He looped the painter through a ring in his landing-stage, climbed up into his hole above, and after a short interval reappeared staggering under a fat, wicker luncheon-basket.

'Shove that under your feet,' he observed to the Mole, as he passed it down into the boat. Then he untied the painter and took the sculls again.

'What's inside it?' asked the Mole, wriggling with curiosity.

'There's cold chicken inside it,' replied the Rat briefly; 'cold tonguecoldhamcoldbeefpickledgherkinssaladfrenchrollscress sandwichespottedmeatgingerbeerlemonadesodawater—'

'O stop, stop,' cried the Mole in ecstacies: 'This is too much!'

'Do you really think so?' enquired the Rat seriously. 'It's only what I always take on these little excursions; and the other animals are always telling me that I'm a mean beast and cut it *very* fine!'

The Mole never heard a word he was saying. Absorbed in the new life he was entering upon, intoxicated with the sparkle, the ripple, the scents and the sounds and the sunlight, he trailed a paw in the water and dreamed long waking dreams. The Water Rat, like the good little fellow he was, sculled steadily on and forebore to disturb him.

'I like your clothes awfully, old chap,' he remarked after some half an hour or so had passed. 'I'm going to get a black velvet smoking-suit myself some day, as soon as I can afford it.'

'I beg your pardon,' said the Mole, pulling himself together with an effort. 'You must think me very rude; but all this is so new to me. So – this – is – a – River!'

'*The* River,' corrected the Rat.

'And you really live by the river? What a jolly life!'

'By it and with it and on it and in it,' said the Rat. 'It's brother and sister to me, and aunts, and company, and food and drink, and (naturally) washing. It's my world, and I don't want any other. What it hasn't got is not worth having, and what it doesn't know is not worth knowing. Lord! the times we've had together! Whether in winter or summer, spring or autumn, it's always got its fun and its excitements. When the floods are on in February, and my cellars and basement are brimming with drink that's no good to me, and the brown water runs by my best bedroom window; or again when it all drops away and shows patches of mud that smells like plum-cake, and the rushes and weed clog the channels, and I can potter about dry-shod over most of the bed of it and find fresh food to eat, and things careless people have dropped out of boats!'

'But isn't it a bit dull at times?' the Mole ventured to ask. 'Just you and the river, and no one else to pass a word with?'

'No one else to – well, I mustn't be hard on you,' said the Rat with forbearance. 'You're new to it, and of course you don't know. The bank is so crowded nowadays that many people are moving away altogether. O no, it isn't what it used to be, at all. Otters, kingfishers, dabchicks, moorhens, all of them about all day long and always wanting you to *do* something – as if a fellow had no business of his own to attend to!'

'What lies over *there?*' asked the Mole, waving a paw towards a background of woodland that darkly framed the water-meadows on one side of the river.

'That? O, that's just the Wild Wood,' said the Rat shortly. 'We don't go there very much, we river-bankers.'

'Aren't they – aren't they very *nice* people in there?' said the Mole, a trifle nervously.

'W-e-ll,' replied the Rat, 'let me see. The squirrels are all right. *And* the rabbits – some of 'em, but rabbits are a mixed lot. And then there's Badger, of course. He lives right in the heart of it; wouldn't live anywhere else, either, if you paid him to do it. Dear old Badger! Nobody interferes with *him*. They'd better not,' he added significantly.

'Why, who *should* interfere with him?' asked the Mole.

'Well, of course – there – are others,' explained the Rat in a hesitating sort of way.

'Weasels – and stoats – and foxes – and so on. They're all right in a way – I'm very good friends with them – pass the time of day when we meet, and all that – but they break out sometimes, there's no denying it, and then – well, you can't really trust them, and that's the fact.'

The Mole knew well that it is quite against animal-etiquette to dwell on possible trouble ahead, or even to allude to it; so he dropped the subject.

'And beyond the Wild Wood again?' he asked: 'Where it's all blue and dim, and one sees what may be hills or perhaps they mayn't, and something like the smoke of towns, or is it only cloud-drift?'

'Beyond the Wild Wood comes the Wide World,' said the Rat. 'And that's something that doesn't matter, either to you or me. I've never been there, and I'm never going, nor you either, if you've got any sense at all. Don't ever refer to it again, please. Now then! Here's our backwater at last, where we're going to lunch.'

Leaving the main stream, they now passed into what seemed at first sight like a little land-locked lake. Green turf sloped down to either edge, brown snaky tree-roots gleamed below the surface of the quiet water, while ahead of them the silvery shoulder and foamy tumble of a weir, arm-in-arm with a restless dripping mill-wheel, that held up in its turn a grey-gabled mill-house, filled the air with a soothing murmur of sound, dull and smothery, yet with little clear voices speaking up cheerfully out of it at intervals. It was so very beautiful that the Mole could only hold up both forepaws and gasp, 'O my! O my! O my!'

The Rat brought the boat alongside the bank, made her fast, helped the still awkward Mole safely ashore, and swung out the luncheon-basket. The Mole begged as a favour to be allowed to unpack it all by himself; and the Rat was very pleased to indulge him, and to sprawl at full length on the grass and rest, while his excited friend shook out the table-cloth and spread it, took out all the mysterious packets one by one and arranged their contents in due order, still gasping, 'O my! O my!' at each fresh revelation. When all was ready, the Rat said, 'Now, pitch in, old fellow!' and the Mole was indeed very glad to obey, for he had started his spring-cleaning at a very early hour that morning, as people *will* do, and had not paused for bite or sup; and he had been through a very great deal since that distant time which now seemed so many days ago.

'What are you looking at?' said the Rat presently, when the edge of their hunger was somewhat dulled, and the Mole's eyes were able to wander off the table-cloth a little.

'I am looking,' said the Mole, 'at a streak of bubbles that I see travelling along the surface of the water. That is a thing that strikes me as funny.'

'Bubbles? Oho!' said the Rat, and chirruped cheerily in an inviting sort of way.

A broad glistening muzzle showed itself above the edge of the bank, and the Otter hauled himself out and shook the water from his coat.

'Greedy beggars!' he observed, making for the provender. 'Why didn't you invite me, Ratty?'

'This was an impromptu affair,' explained the Rat. 'By the way – my friend Mr Mole.'

'Proud, I'm sure,' said the Otter, and the two animals were friends forthwith.

'Such a rumpus everywhere!' continued the Otter. 'All the world seems out on the river to-day. I came up this backwater to try and get a moment's peace, and then stumble upon you fellows! At least – I beg pardon – I don't exactly mean that, you know.'

There was a rustle behind them, proceeding from a hedge wherein last year's leaves still clung thick, and a stripy head, with high shoulders behind it, peered forth on them.

'Come on, old Badger!' shouted the Rat.

The Badger trotted forward a pace or two; then grunted, 'H'm! Company,' and turned his back and disappeared from view.

'That's *just* the sort of fellow he is!' observed the disappointed Rat. 'Simply hates Society! Now we shan't see any more of him to-day. Well, tell us, *who's* out on the river?'

'Toad's out, for one,' replied the Otter. 'In his brand-new wager-boat; new togs, new everything!'

The two animals looked at each other and laughed.

'Once, it was nothing but sailing,' said the Rat. 'Then he tired of that and took to punting. Nothing would please him but to punt all day and every day, and a nice mess he made of it. Last year it was house-boating, and we all had to go and stay with him in his house-boat, and pretend we liked it. He was going to spend the rest of his life in a house-boat. It's all the same, whatever he takes up; he gets tired of it, and starts on something fresh.'

'Such a good fellow, too,' remarked the Otter reflectively. 'But no stability – especially in a boat!'

From where they sat they could get a glimpse of the main stream across the island that separated them; and just then a wager-boat flashed into view, the rower – a short, stout figure – splashing badly and rolling a good deal, but working his hardest. The Rat stood up and hailed him, but Toad – for it was he – shook his head and settled sternly to his work.

'He'll be out of the boat in a minute if he rolls like that,' said the Rat, sitting down again.

'Of course he will,' chuckled the Otter. 'Did I ever tell you that good story about Toad and the lock-keeper? It happened this way. Toad . . .'

An errant May-fly swerved unsteadily athwart the current in the intoxicated fashion affected by young bloods of May-flies seeing life. A swirl of water and a 'cloop!' and the May-fly was visible no more.

Neither was the Otter.

The Mole looked down. The voice was still in his ears, but the turf whereon he had sprawled was clearly vacant. Not an Otter to be seen, as far as the distant horizon.

But again there was a streak of bubbles on the surface of the river.

The Rat hummed a tune, and the Mole recollected that animal-etiquette forbade any sort of comment on the sudden disappearance of one's friends at any moment, for any reason or no reason whatever.

'Well, well,' said the Rat, 'I suppose we ought to be moving. I wonder which of us had better pack the luncheon-basket?' He did not speak as if he was frightfully eager for the treat.

'O, please let me,' said the Mole. So, of course, the Rat let him.

Packing the basket was not quite such pleasant work as unpacking the basket. It never is. But the Mole was bent on enjoying everything, and although just when he had got the basket packed and strapped up tightly he saw a plate staring up at him from the grass, and when the job had been done again the Rat pointed out a fork which anybody ought to have seen, and last of all, behold! the mustard pot, which he had been sitting on without knowing it – still, somehow, the thing got finished at last, without much loss of temper.

The afternoon sun was getting low as the Rat sculled gently homewards in a dreamy mood, murmuring poetry-things over to himself, and not paying much attention to Mole. But the Mole was very full of lunch, and self-satisfaction, and pride, and already quite at home in a boat (so he thought) and was getting a bit restless besides: and presently he said, 'Ratty! Please, *I* want to row, now!'

The Rat shook his head with a smile. 'Not yet, my young friend,' he said – 'wait till you've had a few lessons. It's not so easy as it looks.'

The Mole was quiet for a minute or two. But he began to feel more and more jealous of Rat, sculling so strongly and so easily along, and his pride began to whisper that he could do it every bit as well. He jumped up and seized the sculls, so suddenly, that the Rat, who was gazing out over the water and saying more poetry-things to himself, was taken by surprise and fell backwards off his seat with his legs in the air for the second time, while the triumphant Mole took his place and grabbed the sculls with entire confidence.

'Stop it, you *silly* ass!' cried the Rat, from the bottom of the boat. 'You can't do it! You'll have us over!'

The Mole flung his sculls back with a flourish, and made a great dig at the water. He missed the surface altogether, his legs flew up above his head, and he found himself lying on the top of the prostrate Rat. Greatly alarmed, he made a grab at the side of the boat, and the next moment – Sploosh!

Over went the boat, and he found himself struggling in the river.

O my, how cold the water was, and O, how *very* wet it felt. How it sang in his ears as he went down, down, down! How bright and welcome the sun looked as he rose to the surface coughing and spluttering! How black was his despair when he felt himself sinking again! Then a firm paw gripped him by the back of his neck. It was the Rat, and he was evidently laughing – the Mole could *feel* him laughing, right down his arm and through his paw, and so into his – the Mole's – neck.

The Rat got hold of a scull and shoved it under the Mole's arm; then he did the same by the other side of him and, swimming behind, propelled the helpless animal to shore, hauled him out, and set him down on the bank, a squashy, pulpy lump of misery.

When the Rat had rubbed him down a bit, and wrung some of the wet out of him, he said, 'Now, then, old fellow! Trot up and down the towing-path as hard as you can, till you're warm and dry again, while I dive for the luncheon-basket.'

So the dismal Mole, wet without and ashamed within, trotted about till he was fairly dry, while the Rat plunged into the water again, recovered the boat, righted her and made her fast, fetched his floating property to shore by degrees, and finally dived successfully for the luncheon-basket and struggled to land with it.

When all was ready for a start once more, the Mole, limp and dejected, took his seat in the stern of the boat; and as they set off, he said in a low voice, broken with emotion, 'Ratty, my generous friend! I am very sorry indeed for my foolish and ungrateful conduct. My heart quite fails me when I think how I might have lost that beautiful luncheon-basket. Indeed, I have been a complete ass, and I know it. Will you overlook it this once and forgive me, and let things go on as before?'

'That's all right, bless you!' responded the Rat cheerily. 'What's a little wet to a Water Rat? I'm more in the water than out of it most days. Don't you think any more about it; and, look here! I really think you had better come and stop with me for a little time. It's very plain and rough, you know – not like Toad's house at all – but you haven't seen that yet; still, I can make you comfortable. And I'll teach you to row, and to swim, and you'll soon be as handy on the water as any of us.'

The Mole was so touched by his kind manner of speaking that he could find no voice to answer him; and he had to brush away a tear or two with the back of his paw. But the Rat kindly looked in another direction, and presently the Mole's spirits revived again, and he was even able to give some straight back-talk to a couple of moorhens who were sniggering to each other about his bedraggled appearance.

When they got home, the Rat made a bright fire in the parlour, and planted the Mole in an arm-chair in front of it, having fetched down a dressing-gown and slippers for him, and told him river stories till supper-time. Very thrilling stories they were, too, to an earth-dwelling animal like Mole. Stories about weirs, and sudden floods, and leaping pike, and steamers that flung hard bottles – at least bottles were certainly flung, and *from* steamers, so presumably *by* them; and about herons, and how particular they were whom they spoke to; and about adventures down drains, and night-fishings with Otter, or excursions far a-field with Badger. Supper was a most cheerful meal; but very shortly afterwards a terribly sleepy Mole had to be escorted upstairs by his considerate host, to the best bedroom, where he soon laid his head on his pillow in great peace and contentment, knowing that his new-found friend the River was lapping the sill of his window.

This day was only the first of many similar ones for the emancipated Mole, each of them longer and full of interest as the ripening summer moved onward. He learnt to swim and to row, and entered into the joy of running water; and with his ear to the reed-stems he caught, at intervals, something of what the wind went whispering so constantly among them.

A Portrait

GUY DE MAUPASSANT, *trans.* ALBERT MCMASTER *ET AL.*

'**H**ello! there's Milial!' said somebody near me. I looked at the man who had been pointed out as I had been wishing for a long time to meet this Don Juan.

He was no longer young. His grey hair looked a little like those fur bonnets worn by certain Northern peoples, and his long beard, which fell down over his chest, had also somewhat the appearance of fur. He was talking to a lady, leaning toward her, speaking in a low voice and looking at her with an expression full of respect and tenderness.

I knew his life, or at least as much as was known of it. He had loved madly several times, and there had been certain tragedies with which his name had been connected. When I spoke to women who were the loudest in his praise, and asked them whence came this power, they always answered, after thinking for a while: 'I don't know – he has a certain charm about him.'

He was certainly not handsome. He had none of the elegance that we ascribe to conquerors of feminine hearts. I wondered what might be his hidden charm. Was it mental? I never had heard of a clever saying of his. In his glance? Perhaps. Or in his voice? The voices of some beings have a certain irresistible attraction, almost suggesting the flavour of things good to eat. One is hungry for them, and the sound of their words penetrates us like a dainty morsel. A friend was passing. I asked him: 'Do you know Monsieur Milial?'

'Yes.'

'Introduce us.'

A minute later we were shaking hands and talking in the doorway. What he said was correct, agreeable to hear; it contained no irritable thought. The voice was sweet, soft, caressing, musical; but I had heard others much more attractive, much more moving. One listened to him with pleasure, just as one would look at a pretty little brook. No tension of the mind was necessary in order to follow him, no hidden meaning aroused curiosity, no expectation awoke interest. His conversation was rather restful, but it did not awaken in one either a desire to answer, to contradict or to approve, and it was as easy to answer him as it was to listen to him. The response came to the lips of its own accord, as soon as he had finished talking, and phrases turned toward him as if he had naturally aroused them.

One thought soon struck me. I had known him for a quarter of an hour, and it seemed as if he were already one of my old friends, that I had known all about him for a long time; his face, his gestures, his voice, his ideas. Suddenly, after a few minutes of conversation, he seemed already to be installed in my intimacy. All constraint disappeared between us, and, had he so desired, I might have confided in him as one confides only in old friends.

Certainly there was some mystery about him. Those barriers that are closed between most people and that are lowered with time when sympathy, similar tastes, equal intellectual culture and constant intercourse remove constraint – those barriers seemed not to exist between him and me, and no doubt this was the case between him and all people, both men and women, whom fate threw in his path.

After half an hour we parted, promising to see each other often, and he gave me his address after inviting me to take luncheon with him in two days.

I forgot what hour he had stated, and I arrived too soon; he was not yet home. A correct and silent domestic showed me into a beautiful, quiet, softly lighted parlour. I felt comfortable there, at home. How often I have noticed the influence of apartments on the character and on the mind! There are some which make one feel foolish; in others, on the contrary, one always feels lively. Some make us sad, although well lighted and decorated in light-coloured furniture; others cheer us up, although hung with sombre material. Our eye, like our heart, has its likes and dislikes, of which it does not inform us, and which it secretly imposes on our temperament. The harmony of furniture, walls, the style of an ensemble, act immediately on our mental state, just as the air from the woods, the sea or the mountains modifies our physical natures.

I sat down on a cushion-covered divan and felt myself suddenly carried and supported by these little silk bags of feathers, as if the outline of my body had been marked out beforehand on this couch.

Then I looked about. There was nothing striking about the room; everywhere were beautiful and modest things, simple and rare furniture, Oriental curtains which did not seem to come from a department store but from the interior of a harem; and exactly opposite me hung the portrait of a woman. It was a portrait of medium size, showing the head and the upper part of the body, and the hands, which were holding a book. She was young, bareheaded; ribbons were woven in her hair; she was smiling sadly. Was it because she was bareheaded, was it merely her natural expression? I never have seen a portrait of a lady which seemed so much in its place as that one in that dwelling. Of all those I knew I have seen nothing like that one. All those that I know are on exhibition, whether the lady be dressed in her gaudiest gown, with an attractive headdress and a look which shows that she is posing first of all before the artist and then before those who will look at her or whether they have taken a comfortable attitude in an ordinary gown. Some are standing majestically in all their beauty, which is not at all natural to them in life. All of them have something, a flower or a jewel, a crease in the dress or a curve of the lip, which one feels to have been placed there for effect by the artist. Whether they wear a hat or merely their hair one can immediately notice that they are not entirely natural. Why? One cannot say without knowing them, but the effect is there. They seem to be calling somewhere, on people whom they wish to please and to whom they wish to appear at their best advantage; and they have studied their attitudes, sometimes modest, sometimes haughty.

What could one say about this one? She was at home and alone. Yes, she was alone, for she was smiling as one smiles when thinking in solitude of something sad or sweet, and not as one smiles when one is being watched. She seemed so much alone and so much at home that she made the whole large apartment seem absolutely empty. She alone lived in it, filled it, gave it life. Many people might come in and converse, laugh, even sing; she would still be alone with a solitary smile, and she alone would give it life with her pictured gaze.

That look also was unique. It fell directly on me, fixed and caressing, without seeing me. All portraits know that they are being watched, and they answer with their eyes, which see, think, follow us without leaving us, from the very moment we enter the apartment they inhabit. This one did not see me; it saw nothing, although its look was fixed directly on me. I remembered the surprising verse of Baudelaire:

And your eyes, attractive as those of a portrait.

They did indeed attract me in an irresistible manner; those painted eyes which had lived, or which were perhaps still living, threw over me a strange, powerful spell. Oh, what an infinite and tender charm, like a passing breeze, like a dying sunset of lilac rose and blue, a little sad like the approaching night, which comes behind the sombre frame and out of those impenetrable eyes! Those eyes, created by a few strokes from a brush, hide behind them the mystery of that which seems to be and which does not exist, which can appear in the eyes of a woman, which can make love blossom within us.

The door opened and M. Milial entered. He excused himself for being late. I excused myself for being ahead of time. Then I said: 'Might I ask you who is this lady?'

He answered: 'That is my mother. She died very young.'

Then I understood whence came the inexplicable attraction of this man.

The Golden Windows

LAURA E. RICHARDS

All day long the little boy had worked hard, in field and barn and shed, for his people were poor farmers, and could not pay a workman; but at sunset there came an hour that was all his own, for his father had given it to him. Then the boy would go up to the top of a hill and look across at another hill that rose some miles away. On this far hill stood a house with windows of clear gold and diamonds. They shone and blazed so that it made the boy wink to look at them: but after a while the people in the house put up shutters, as it seemed, and then it looked like any common farmhouse. The boy supposed they did this because it was supper-time; and then he would go into the house and have his supper of bread and milk, and so to bed.

One day the boy's father called him and said: 'You have been a good boy, and have earned a holiday. Take this day for your own; but remember that God gave it, and try to learn some good thing.'

The boy thanked his father and kissed his mother; then he put a piece of bread in his pocket, and started off to find the house with the golden windows.

It was pleasant walking. His bare feet made marks in the white dust, and when he looked back, the footprints seemed to be following him, and making company for him. His shadow, too, kept beside him, and would dance or run with him as he pleased; so it was very cheerful.

By and by he felt hungry; and he sat down by a brown brook that ran through the alder hedge by the roadside, and ate his bread, and drank the clear water. Then he scattered the crumbs for the birds, as his mother had taught him to do, and went on his way.

After a long time he came to a high green hill; and when he had climbed the hill, there was the house on the top; but it seemed that the shutters were up, for he could not see the golden windows. He came up to the house, and then he could well have wept, for the windows were of clear glass, like any others, and there was no gold anywhere about them.

A woman came to the door, and looked kindly at the boy, and asked him what he wanted.

'I saw the golden windows from our hilltop,' he said, 'and I came to see them, but now they are only glass.'

The woman shook her head and laughed.

'We are poor farming people,' she said, 'and are not likely to have gold about our windows; but glass is better to see through.'

She bade the boy sit down on the broad stone step at the door, and brought him a cup of milk and a cake, and bade him rest; then she called her daughter, a child of his own age, and nodded kindly at the two, and went back to her work.

The little girl was barefooted like himself, and wore a brown cotton gown, but her hair was golden like the windows he had seen, and her eyes were blue like the sky at noon. She led the boy about the farm, and showed him her black calf with the white star on its forehead, and he told her about his own at home, which was red like a chestnut, with four white feet. Then when they had eaten an apple together, and so had become friends, the boy asked her about the golden windows. The little girl nodded, and said she knew all about them, only he had mistaken the house.

'You have come quite the wrong way!' she said. 'Come with me, and I will show you the house with the golden windows, and then you will see for yourself.'

They went to a knoll that rose behind the farmhouse, and as they went the little girl told him that the golden windows could only be seen at a certain hour, about sunset.

'Yes, I know that!' said the boy.

When they reached the top of the knoll, the girl turned and pointed; and there on a hill far away stood a house with windows of clear gold and diamond, just as he had seen them. And when they looked again, the boy saw that it was his own home.

Then he told the little girl that he must go; and he gave her his best pebble, the white one with the red band, that he had carried for a year in his pocket; and she gave him three horse-chestnuts, one red like satin, one spotted, and one white like milk. He kissed her, and promised to come again, but he did not tell her what he had learned; and so he went back down the hill, and the little girl stood in the sunset light and watched him.

The way home was long, and it was dark before the boy reached his father's house; but the lamplight and firelight shone through the windows, making them almost as bright as he had seen them from the hilltop; and when he opened the door, his mother came to kiss him, and his little sister ran to throw her arms about his neck, and his father looked up and smiled from his seat by the fire.

'Have you had a good day?' asked his mother.

Yes, the boy had had a very good day.

'And have you learned anything?' asked his father.

'Yes!' said the boy. 'I have learned that our house has windows of gold and diamond.'

To Sleep

WILLIAM WORDSWORTH

A FLOCK of sheep that leisurely pass by
One after one; the sound of rain, and bees
Murmuring; the fall of rivers, winds and seas,
Smooth fields, white sheets of water, and pure sky; –

I've thought of all by turns, and still I lie
Sleepless; and soon the small birds' melodies
Must hear, first utter'd from my orchard trees,
And the first cuckoo's melancholy cry.

Even thus last night, and two nights more I lay,
And could not win thee, Sleep! by any stealth:
So do not let me wear to-night away:

Without Thee what is all the morning's wealth?
Come, blessèd barrier between day and day,
Dear mother of fresh thoughts and joyous health!

The Diary of a Nobody *(excerpt)*

GEORGE & WEEDON GROSSMITH

INTRODUCTION BY MR POOTER

*Why should I not publish my diary? I have often seen reminiscences of
people I have never even heard of, and I fail to see – because I do not
happen to be a 'Somebody' – why my diary should not be interesting.
My only regret is that I did not commence it when I was a youth.*

Charles Pooter.

The Laurels,

Brickfield Terrace,

Holloway.

I

We settle down in our new home, and I resolve to keep a diary.
Tradesmen trouble us a bit, so does the scraper. The Curate calls
and pays me a great compliment.

My dear wife Carrie and I have just been a week in our new house, 'The Laurels', Brickfield Terrace, Holloway – a nice six-roomed residence, not counting basement, with a front break-fast-parlour. We have a little front garden; and there is a flight of ten steps up to the front door, which, by-the-by, we keep locked with the chain up. Cummings, Gowing, and our other intimate friends always come to the little side entrance, which saves the servant the trouble of going up to the front door, thereby taking her from her work. We have a nice little back garden which runs down to the railway. We were rather afraid of the noise of the trains at first, but the landlord said we should not notice them after a bit, and took £2 off the rent. He was certainly right; and beyond the cracking of the garden wall at the bottom, we have suffered no inconvenience.

After my work in the City, I like to be at home. What's the good of a home, if you are never in it? 'Home, Sweet Home,' that's my motto. I am always in of an evening. Our old friend Gowing may drop in without ceremony; so may Cummings, who lives opposite. My dear wife Caroline and I are pleased to see them, if they like to drop in on us. But Carrie and I can manage to pass our evenings together without friends. There is always something to be done: a tin-tack here, a Venetian blind to put straight, a fan to nail up, or part of a carpet to nail down – all of which I can do with my pipe in my mouth; while Carrie is not above putting a button on a shirt, mending a pillow-case, or practising the 'Sylvia Gavotte' on our new cottage piano (on the three years' system), manufactured by W. Bilkson (in small letters), from Collard and Collard (in very large letters). It is also a great comfort to us to know that our boy Willie is getting on so well in the Bank at Oldham. We should like to see more of him. Now for my diary: –

April 3. – Tradesmen called for custom, and I promised Farmerson, the ironmonger, to give him a turn if I wanted any nails or tools. By-the-by, that reminds me there is no key to our bedroom door, and the bells must be seen to. The parlour bell is broken, and the front door rings up in the servant's bedroom, which is ridiculous. Dear friend Gowing dropped in, but wouldn't stay, saying there was an infernal smell of paint.

April 4. Tradesmen still calling; Carrie being out, I arranged to deal with Horwin, who seemed a civil butcher with a nice clean shop. Ordered a shoulder of mutton for to-morrow, to give him a trial. Carrie arranged with Borset, the butterman, and ordered a pound of fresh butter, and a pound and a half of salt ditto for kitchen, and a shilling's worth of eggs. In the evening, Cummings unexpectedly dropped in to show me a meerschaum pipe he had won in a raffle in the City, and told me to handle it carefully, as it would spoil the colouring if the hand was moist. He said he wouldn't stay, as he didn't care much for the smell of the paint, and fell over the scraper as he went out. Must get the scraper removed, or else I shall get into a *scrape*. I don't often make jokes.

April 5. – Two shoulders of mutton arrived, Carrie having arranged with another butcher without consulting me. Gowing called, and fell over scraper coming in. *Must* get that scraper removed.

April 6. – Eggs for breakfast simply shocking; sent them back to Borset with my compliments, and he needn't call any more for orders. Couldn't find umbrella, and though it was pouring with rain, had to go without it. Sarah said Mr Gowing must have took it by mistake last night, as there was a stick in the 'all that didn't belong to nobody. In the evening, hearing someone talking in a loud voice to the servant in the downstairs hall, I went out to see who it was, and was surprised to find it was Borset, the butterman, who was both drunk and offensive. Borset, on seeing me, said he would be hanged if he would ever serve City clerks any more – the game wasn't worth the candle. I restrained my feelings, and quietly remarked that I thought it was *possible* for a city clerk to be a *gentleman*. He replied he was very glad to hear it, and wanted to know whether I had ever come across one, for *he* hadn't. He left the house, slamming the door after him, which nearly broke the fanlight; and I heard him fall over the scraper, which made me feel glad I hadn't removed it. When he had gone, I thought of a splendid answer I ought to have given him. However, I will keep it for another occasion.

April 7. – Being Saturday, I looked forward to being home early, and putting a few things straight; but two of our principals at the office were absent through illness, and I did not get home till seven. Found Borset waiting. He had been three times during the day to apologise for his conduct last night. He said he was unable to take his Bank Holiday last Monday, and took it last night instead. He begged me to accept his apology, and a pound of fresh butter. He seems, after all, a decent sort of fellow; so I gave him an order for some fresh eggs, with a request that on this occasion they *should* be fresh. I am afraid we shall have to get some new stair-carpets after all; our old ones are not quite wide enough to meet the paint on either side. Carrie suggests that we might ourselves broaden the paint. I will see if we can match the colour (dark chocolate) on Monday.

April 8, Sunday. – After Church, the Curate came back with us. I sent Carrie in to open front door, which we do not use except on special occasions. She could not get it open, and after all my display, I had to take the Curate (whose name, by-the-by, I did not catch) round the side entrance. He caught his foot in the scraper, and tore the bottom of his trousers. Most annoying, as Carrie could not well offer to repair them on a Sunday. After dinner, went to sleep. Took a walk round the garden, and discovered a beautiful spot for sowing mustard-and-cress and radishes. Went to Church again in the evening: walked back with the Curate. Carrie noticed he had got on the same pair of trousers, only repaired. He wants me to take round the plate, which I think a great compliment.

II

Tradesmen and the scraper still troublesome. Growing rather tiresome with his complaints of the paint. I make one of the best jokes of my life. Delights of Gardening. Mr Stillbrook, Gowing, Cummings, and I have a little misunderstanding. Sarah makes me look a fool before Cummings.

April 9. – Commenced the morning badly. The butcher, whom we decided *not* to arrange with, called and blackguarded me in the most uncalled-for manner. He began by abusing me, and saying he did not want my custom. I simply said: 'Then what are you making all this fuss about it for?' And he shouted out at the top of his voice, so that all the neighbours could hear: 'Pah! go along. Ugh! I could buy up "things" like you by the dozen!'

I shut the door, and was giving Carrie to understand that this disgraceful scene was entirely her fault, when there was a violent kicking at the door, enough to break the panels. It was the black-guard butcher again, who said he had cut his foot over the scraper, and would immediately bring an action against me. Called at Farmerson's, the ironmonger, on my way to town, and gave him the job of moving the scraper and repairing the bells, thinking it scarcely worth while to trouble the landlord with such a trifling matter.

Arrived home tired and worried. Mr Putley, a painter and decorator, who had sent in a card, said he could not match the colour on the stairs, as it contained Indian carmine. He said he spent half-a-day calling at warehouses to see if he could get it. He suggested he should entirely repaint the stairs. It would cost very little more; if he tried to match it, he could only make a bad job of it. It would be more satisfactory to him and to us to have the work done properly. I consented, but felt I had been talked over. Planted some mustard-and-cress and radishes, and went to bed at nine.

April 10. – Farmerson came round to attend to the scraper himself. He seems a very civil fellow. He says he does not usually conduct such small jobs personally, but for me he would do so. I thanked him, and went to town. It is disgraceful how late some of the young clerks are at arriving. I told three of them that if Mr Perkupp, the principal, heard of it, they might be discharged.

Pitt, a monkey of seventeen, who has only been with us six weeks, told me 'to keep my hair on!' I informed him I had had the honour of being in the firm twenty years, to which he insolently replied that I 'looked it.' I gave him an indignant look, and said: 'I demand from you some respect, sir.' He replied: 'All right, go on demanding.' I would not argue with him any further. You cannot argue with people like that. In the evening Gowing called, and repeated his complaint about the smell of paint. Gowing is sometimes very tedious with his remarks, and not always cautious; and Carrie once very properly reminded him that she was present.

April 11. – Mustard-and-cress and radishes not come up yet. To-day was a day of annoyances. I missed the quarter-to-nine 'bus to the City, through having words with the grocer's boy, who for the second time had the impertinence to bring his basket to the hall-door, and had left the marks of his dirty boots on the fresh-cleaned door-steps. He said he had knocked at the side door with his knuckles for a quarter of an hour. I knew Sarah, our servant, could not hear this, as she was upstairs doing the bedrooms, so asked the boy why he did not ring the bell? He replied that he did pull the bell, but the handle came off in his hand.

I was half-an-hour late at the office, a thing that has never happened to me before. There has recently been much irregularity in the attendance of the clerks, and Mr Perkupp, our principal, unfortunately choose this very morning to pounce down upon us early. Someone had given the tip to the others. The result was that I was the only one late of the lot. Buckling, one of the senior clerks, was a brick, and I was saved by his intervention. As I passed by Pitt's desk, I heard him remark to his neighbour: 'How disgracefully late some of the head clerks arrive!' This was, of course, meant for me. I treated the observation with silence, simply giving him a look, which unfortunately had the effect of making both of the clerks laugh. Thought afterwards it would have been more dignified if I had pretended not to have heard him at all. Cummings called in the evening, and we played dominoes.

April 12. – Mustard-and-cress and radishes not come up yet. Left Farmerson repairing the scraper, but when I came home found three men working. I asked the meaning of it, and Farmerson said that in making a fresh hole he had penetrated the gas-pipe. He said it was a most ridiculous place to put the gas-pipe, and the man who did it evidently knew nothing about his business. I felt his excuse was no consolation for the expense I shall be put to.

In the evening, after tea, Gowing dropped in, and we had a smoke together in the breakfast-parlour. Carrie joined us later, but did not stay long, saying the smoke was too much for her. It was also rather too much for me, for Gowing had given me what he called a green cigar, one that his friend Shoemach had just brought over from America. The cigar didn't look green, but I fancy I must have done so; for when I had smoked a little more than half I was obliged to retire on the pretext of telling Sarah to bring in the glasses.

I took a walk round the garden three or four times, feeling the need of fresh air. On returning Gowing noticed I was not smoking: offered me another cigar, which I politely declined. Gowing began his usual sniffing, so, anticipating him, I said: 'You're not going to complain of the smell of paint again?' He said: 'No, not this time; but I'll tell you what, I distinctly smell dry rot.' I don't often make jokes, but I replied: 'You're talking a lot of *dry rot* yourself.' I could not help roaring at this, and Carrie said her sides quite ached with laughter. I never was so immensely tickled by anything I have ever said before. I actually woke up twice during the night, and laughed till the bed shook.

April 13. – An extraordinary coincidence: Carrie had called in a woman to make some chintz covers for our drawing-room chairs and sofa to prevent the sun fading the green rep of the furniture. I saw the woman, and recognised her as a woman who used to work years ago for my old aunt at Clapham. It only shows how small the world is.

April 14. – Spent the whole of the afternoon in the garden, having this morning picked up at a bookstall for fivepence a capital little book, in good condition, on *Gardening*. I procured and sowed some half-hardy annuals in what I fancy will be a warm, sunny border. I thought of a joke, and called out Carrie. Carrie came out rather testy, I thought. I said: 'I have just discovered we have got a lodging-house.' She replied: 'How do you mean?' I said: 'Look at the *boarders*.' Carrie said: 'Is that all you wanted me for?' I said: 'Any other time you would have laughed at my little pleasantry.' Carrie said: 'Certainly – *at any other time*, but not when I am busy in the house.' The stairs looked very nice. Gowing called, and said the stairs looked *all right*, but it made the banisters look *all wrong*, and suggested a coat of paint on them also, which Carrie quite agreed with. I walked round to Putley, and fortunately he was out, so I had a good excuse to let the banisters slide. By-the-by, that is rather funny.

The Drawing of the Sword

ANDREW LANG

*L*ong, long ago, after Uther Pendragon died, there was no
King in Britain, and every Knight hoped to seize the crown
for himself. The country was like to fare ill when laws were
broken on every side, and the corn which was to give the poor
bread was trodden underfoot, and there was none to bring the
evildoer to justice. Then, when things were at their worst, came
forth Merlin the magician, and fast he rode to the place where
the Archbishop of Canterbury had his dwelling. And they took
counsel together, and agreed that all the lords and gentlemen of
Britain should ride to London and meet on Christmas Day, now
at hand, in the Great Church. So this was done. And on Christmas
morning, as they left the church, they saw in the churchyard a
large stone, and on it a bar of steel, and in the steel a naked
sword was held, and about it was written in letters of gold,
'Whoso pulleth out this sword is by right of birth King of
England.' They marvelled at these words, and called for the
Archbishop, and brought him into the place where the stone
stood. Then those Knights who fain would be King could not

hold themselves back, and they tugged at the sword with all their might; but it never stirred. The Archbishop watched them in silence, but when they were faint from pulling he spoke: 'The man is not here who shall lift out that sword, nor do I know where to find him. But this is my counsel – that two Knights be chosen, good and true men, to keep guard over the sword.'

Thus it was done. But the lords and gentlemen-at-arms cried out that every man had a right to try to win the sword, and they decided that on New Year's Day a tournament should be held, and any Knight who would, might enter the lists.

So on New Year's Day, the Knights, as their custom was, went to hear service in the Great Church, and after it was over they met in the field to make ready for the tourney. Among them was a brave Knight called Sir Ector, who brought with him Sir Kay, his son, and Arthur, Kay's foster-brother. Now Kay had unbuckled his sword the evening before, and in his haste to be at the tourney had forgotten to put it on again, and he begged Arthur to ride back and fetch it for him. But when Arthur reached the house the door was locked, for the women had gone out to see the tourney, and though Arthur tried his best to get in he could not. Then he rode away in great anger, and said to himself, 'Kay shall not be without a sword this day. I will take that sword in the churchyard, and give it to him'; and he galloped fast till he reached the gate of the churchyard. Here he jumped down and tied his horse tightly to a tree, then, running up to the stone, he seized the handle of the sword, and drew it easily out; afterwards he mounted his horse again, and delivered the sword to Sir Kay. The moment Sir Kay saw the sword he knew it was not his own, but the sword of the stone, and he sought out his father Sir Ector, and said to him, 'Sir, this is the sword of the stone, therefore I am the rightful King.' Sir Ector made no answer, but signed to Kay and Arthur to follow him, and they all three went back to the church. Leaving their horses outside, they entered the choir, and here Sir Ector took a holy book and bade Sir Kay swear how he came by that sword. 'My brother Arthur gave it to me,' replied Sir Kay. 'How did you come by it?' asked Sir Ector, turning to Arthur. 'Sir,' said Arthur, 'when I rode home for my brother's sword I found no one to deliver it to me, and as I resolved he should not be swordless I thought of the sword in this stone, and I pulled it out.' 'Were any Knights present when you did this?' asked Sir Ector. 'No, none,' said Arthur. 'Then it is you,' said Sir Ector, 'who are the rightful King of this land.' 'But why am I the King?' inquired Arthur. 'Because,' answered Sir Ector, 'this is an enchanted sword, and no man could draw it but he who was born a King. Therefore put the sword back into the stone, and let me see you take it out.' 'That is soon done,' said Arthur, replacing the sword, and Sir Ector himself tried to draw it, but he could not. 'Now it is your turn,' he said to Sir Kay, but Sir Kay fared no better than his father, though he tugged with all his might and main. 'Now you, Arthur,' and Arthur pulled it out as easily as if it had been lying in its sheath, and as he did so Sir Ector and Sir Kay sank on their knees before him. 'Why do you, my father and brother, kneel to me?' asked Arthur in surprise. 'Nay, nay, my lord,' answered Sir Ector, 'I was never your father, though till to-day I did not know who your father really was. You are the son of Uther Pendragon, and you were brought to me when you were born by Merlin himself, who promised that when the time came I should know from whom you sprang. And now it has been revealed to me.' But when Arthur heard that Sir Ector was not his father, he wept bitterly. 'If I am King,' he said at last, I ask what you will, and I shall not fail you. For to you, and to my lady and mother, I owe more than to anyone in the world, for she loved me and treated me as her son.' 'Sir,' replied Sir Ector, 'I only ask that you will make your foster-brother, Sir Kay, Seneschal of all your lands.' 'That I will readily,' answered Arthur, 'and while he and I live no other shall fill that office.'

Sir Ector then bade them seek out the Archbishop with him, and they told him all that had happened concerning the sword, which Arthur had left standing in the stone. And on the Twelfth Day the Knights and Barons came again, but none could draw it out but Arthur. When they saw this, many of the Barons became angry and cried out that they would never own a boy for King whose blood was no better than their own. So it was agreed to wait till Candlemas, when more Knights might be there, and meanwhile the same two men who had been chosen before watched the sword night and day; but at Candlemas it was the same thing, and at Easter. And when Pentecost came, the common people who were present, and saw Arthur pull out the sword, cried with one voice that he was their King, and they would kill any man who said differently. Then rich and poor fell on their knees before him, and Arthur took the sword and offered it upon the altar where the Archbishop stood, and the best man that was there made him Knight. After that the crown was put on his head, and he swore to his lords and commons that he would be a true King, and would do them justice all the days of his life.

The Tiredness of Rosabel

KATHERINE MANSFIELD

At the corner of Oxford Circus Rosabel bought a bunch of violets, and that was practically the reason why she had so little tea – for a scone and a boiled egg and a cup of cocoa at Lyons are not ample sufficiency after a hard day's work in a millinery establishment. As she swung on to the step of the Atlas 'bus, grabbed her skirt with one hand and clung to the railing with the other, Rosabel thought she would have sacrificed her soul for a good dinner – roast duck and green peas, chestnut stuffing, pudding with brandy sauce – something hot and strong and filling. She sat down next to a girl very much her own age who was reading *Anna Lombard* in a cheap, paper-covered edition, and the rain had tear-spattered the pages. Rosabel looked out of the windows; the street was blurred and misty, but light striking on the panes turned their dullness to opal and silver, and the jewellers' shops seen through this, were fairy palaces. Her feet were horribly wet, and she knew the bottom of her skirt and petticoat would be coated with black, greasy mud. There was a sickening smell of warm humanity – it seemed to be oozing out of everybody in the 'bus – and everybody had the same expression, sitting so still, staring in front of them. How many times had she read these advertisements – 'Sapolio Saves Time, Saves Labour' – 'Heinz's Tomato Sauce' – and the inane, annoying dialogue between doctor and judge concerning the superlative merits of 'Lamplough's Pyretic Saline'. She glanced at the book which the girl read so earnestly, mouthing the words in a way that Rosabel detested, licking her first finger and thumb each time that she turned the page. She could not see very clearly; it was something about a hot, voluptuous night, a band playing, and a girl with lovely, white shoulders. Oh, Heavens! Rosabel stirred suddenly and unfastened the two top buttons of her coat . . . she felt almost stifled. Through her half-closed eyes the whole row of people on the opposite seat seemed to resolve into one fatuous, staring face . . .

And this was her corner. She stumbled a little on her way out and lurched against the girl next her. 'I beg your pardon,' said Rosabel, but the girl did not even look up. Rosabel saw that she was smiling as she read.

Westbourne Grove looked as she had always imagined Venice to look at night, mysterious, dark, even the hansoms were like gondolas dodging up and down, and the lights trailing luridly – tongues of flame licking the wet street – magic fish swimming in the Grand Canal. She was more than glad to reach Richmond Road, but from the corner of the street until she came to No. 26 she thought of those four flights of stairs. Oh, why four flights! It was really criminal to expect people to live so high up. Every house ought to have a lift, something simple and inexpensive, or else an electric staircase like the one at Earl's Court – but four flights! When she stood in the hall and saw the first flight ahead of her and the stuffed albatross head on the landing, glimmering ghost-like in the light of the little gas jet, she almost cried. Well, they had to be faced; it was very like bicycling up a steep hill, but there was not the satisfaction of flying down the other side . . .

Her own room at last! She closed the door, lit the gas, took off her hat and coat, skirt, blouse, unhooked her old flannel dressing-gown from behind the door, pulled it on, then unlaced her boots – on consideration her stockings were not wet enough to change. She went over to the wash-stand. The jug had not been filled again to-day. There was just enough water to soak the sponge, and the enamel was coming off the basin – that was the second time she had scratched her chin.

It was just seven o'clock. If she pulled the blind up and put out the gas it was much more restful – Rosabel did not want to read. So she knelt down on the floor, pillowing her arms on the window-sill . . . just one little sheet of glass between her and the great wet world outside!

She began to think of all that had happened during the day. Would she ever forget that awful woman in the grey mackintosh who had wanted a trimmed motor-cap – 'something purple with something rosy each side' – or the girl who had tried on every hat in the shop and then said she would 'call in to-morrow and decide definitely.' Rosabel could not help smiling; the excuse was worn so thin . . .

But there had been one other – a girl with beautiful red hair and a white skin and eyes the colour of that green ribbon shot with gold they had got from Paris last week. Rosabel had seen her electric brougham at the door; a man had come in with her, quite a young man, and so well dressed.

'What is it exactly that I want, Harry?' she had said, as Rosabel took the pins out of her hat, untied her veil, and gave her a hand-mirror.

'You must have a black hat,' he had answered, 'a black hat with a feather that goes right round it and then round your neck and ties in a bow under your chin, and the ends tuck into your belt – a decent-sized feather.'

The girl glanced at Rosabel laughingly. 'Have you any hats like that?'

They had been very hard to please; Harry would demand the impossible, and Rosabel was almost in despair. Then she remembered the big, untouched box upstairs.

'Oh, one moment, Madam,' she had said. 'I think perhaps I can show you something that will please you better.' She had run up, breathlessly, cut the cords, scattered the tissue paper, and yes, there was the very hat – rather large, soft, with a great, curled feather, and a black velvet rose, nothing else. They had been charmed. The girl had put it on and then handed it to Rosabel.

'Let me see how it looks on you,' she said, frowning a little, very serious indeed.

Rosabel turned to the mirror and placed it on her brown hair, then faced them.

'Oh, Harry, isn't it adorable,' the girl cried, 'I must have that!' She smiled again at Rosabel. 'It suits you, beautifully.'

A sudden, ridiculous feeling of anger had seized Rosabel. She longed to throw the lovely, perishable thing in the girl's face, and bent over the hat, flushing.

'It's exquisitely finished off inside, Madam,' she said. The girl swept out to her brougham, and left Harry to pay and bring the box with him.

'I shall go straight home and put it on before I come out to lunch with you,' Rosabel heard her say.

The man leant over her as she made out the bill, then, as he counted the money into her hand – 'Ever been painted?' he said.

'No,' said Rosabel, shortly, realising the swift change in his voice, the slight tinge of insolence, of familiarity.

'Oh, well you ought to be,' said Harry. 'You've got such a damned pretty little figure.'

Rosabel did not pay the slightest attention. How handsome he had been! She had thought of no one else all day; his face fascinated her; she could see clearly his fine, straight eyebrows, and his hair grew back from his forehead with just the slightest suspicion of crisp curl, his laughing, disdainful mouth. She saw again his slim hands counting the money into hers . . . Rosabel suddenly pushed the hair back from her face, her forehead was hot . . . if those slim hands could rest one moment . . . the luck of that girl!

Suppose they changed places. Rosabel would drive home with him, of course they were in love with each other, but not engaged, very nearly, and she would say – 'I won't be one moment.' He would wait in the brougham while her maid took the hat-box up the stairs, following Rosabel. Then the great, white and pink bedroom with roses everywhere in dull silver vases. She would sit down before the mirror and the little French maid would fasten her hat and find her a thin, fine veil and another pair of white suède gloves – a button had come off the gloves she had worn that morning. She had scented her furs and gloves and handkerchief, taken a big muff and run down stairs. The butler opened the door, Harry was waiting, they drove away together . . . *That was life*, thought Rosabel! On the way to the Carlton they stopped at Gerard's, Harry bought her great sprays of Parma violets, filled her hands with them.

'Oh, they are sweet!' she said, holding them against her face.

'It is as you always should be,' said Harry, 'with your hands full of violets.'

(Rosabel realised that her knees were getting stiff; she sat down on the floor and leant her head against the wall.) Oh, that lunch! The table covered with flowers, a band hidden behind a grove of palms playing music that fired her blood like wine – the soup, and oysters, and pigeons, and creamed potatoes, and champagne, of course, and afterwards coffee and cigarettes. She would lean over the table fingering her glass with one hand, talking with that charming gaiety which Harry so appreciated. Afterwards a matinée, something that gripped them both, and then tea at the 'Cottage'.

'Sugar? Milk? Cream?' The little homely questions seemed to suggest a joyous intimacy. And then home again in the dusk, and the scent of the Parma violets seemed to drench the air with their sweetness.

'I'll call for you at nine,' he said as he left her.

The fire had been lighted in her boudoir, the curtains drawn, there were a great pile of letters waiting her – invitations for the

Opera, dinners, balls, a week-end on the river, a motor tour – she glanced through them listlessly as she went upstairs to dress. A fire in her bedroom, too, and her beautiful, shining dress spread on the bed – white tulle over silver, silver shoes, silver scarf, a little silver fan. Rosabel knew that she was the most famous woman at the ball that night; men paid her homage, a foreign Prince desired to be presented to this English wonder. Yes, it was a voluptuous night, a band playing, and *her* lovely white shoulders . . .

But she became very tired. Harry took her home, and came in with her for just one moment. The fire was out in the drawing room, but the sleepy maid waited for her in her boudoir. She took off her cloak, dismissed the servant, and went over to the fireplace, and stood peeling off her gloves; the firelight shone on her hair, Harry came across the room and caught her in his arms – 'Rosabel, Rosabel, Rosabel' . . . Oh, the haven of those arms, and she was very tired.

(The real Rosabel, the girl crouched on the floor in the dark, laughed aloud, and put her hand up to her hot mouth.)

Of course they rode in the park next morning, the engagement had been announced in the *Court Circular*, all the world knew, all the world was shaking hands with her . . .

They were married shortly afterwards at St George's, Hanover Square, and motored down to Harry's old ancestral home for the honeymoon; the peasants in the village curtseyed to them as they passed; under the folds of the rug he pressed her hands convulsively. And that night she wore again her white and silver frock. She was tired after the journey and went upstairs to bed . . . quite early . . .

The real Rosabel got up from the floor and undressed slowly, folding her clothes over the back of a chair. She slipped over her head her coarse, calico nightdress, and took the pins out of her hair – the soft, brown flood of it fell round her, warmly. Then she blew out the candle and groped her way into bed, pulling the blankets and grimy 'honeycomb' quilt closely round her neck, cuddling down in the darkness . . .

So she slept and dreamed, and smiled in her sleep, and once threw out her arm to feel for something which was not there, dreaming still.

And the night passed. Presently the cold fingers of dawn closed over her uncovered hand; grey light flooded the dull room. Rosabel shivered, drew a little gasping breath, sat up. And because her heritage was that tragic optimism, which is all too often the only inheritance of youth, still half asleep, she smiled, with a little nervous tremor round her mouth.

Clouds

CHRISTINA ROSSETTI

White sheep, white sheep,
On a blue hill,
When the wind stops,
You all stand still.
When the wind blows,
You walk away slow.
White sheep, white sheep,
Where do you go?

The Beauties

ANTON CHEKHOV, *trans.* CONSTANCE GARNETT

I

I remember, when I was a high school boy in the fifth or sixth class, I was driving with my grandfather from the village of Bolshoe Kryepkoe in the Don region to Rostov-on-the-Don. It was a sultry, languidly dreary day of August. Our eyes were glued together, and our mouths were parched from the heat and the dry burning wind which drove clouds of dust to meet us; one did not want to look or speak or think, and when our drowsy driver, a Little Russian called Karpo, swung his whip at the horses and lashed me on my cap, I did not protest or utter a sound, but only, rousing myself from half-slumber, gazed mildly and dejectedly into the distance to see whether there was a village visible through the dust. We stopped to feed the horses in a big Armenian village at a rich Armenian's whom my grandfather knew. Never in my life have I seen a greater caricature than that Armenian. Imagine a little shaven head with thick overhanging eyebrows, a beak of a nose, long grey moustaches, and a wide mouth with a long cherry-wood chibouk sticking out of it. This little head was clumsily attached to a lean hunch-back carcass attired in a fantastic garb, a short red jacket, and full bright blue trousers. This figure walked straddling its legs and shuffling with its slippers, spoke without taking the chibouk out of its mouth, and behaved with truly Armenian dignity, not smiling, but staring with wide-open eyes and trying to take as little notice as possible of its guests.

There was neither wind nor dust in the Armenian's rooms, but it was just as unpleasant, stifling, and dreary as in the steppe and on the road. I remember, dusty and exhausted by the heat, I sat in the corner on a green box. The unpainted wooden walls, the furniture, and the floors coloured with yellow ochre smelt of dry wood baked by the sun. Wherever I looked there were flies and flies and flies . . . Grandfather and the Armenian were talking about grazing, about manure, and about oats . . . I knew that they would be a good hour getting the samovar; that grandfather would be not less than an hour drinking his tea, and then would lie down to sleep for two or three hours; that I should waste a quarter of the day waiting, after which there would be again the heat, the dust, the jolting cart. I heard the muttering of the two voices, and it began to seem to me that I had been seeing the Armenian, the cupboard with the crockery, the flies, the windows with the burning sun beating on them, for ages and ages, and should only cease to see them in the far-off future, and I was seized with hatred for the steppe, the sun, the flies . . .

A Little Russian peasant woman in a kerchief brought in a tray of tea-things, then the samovar. The Armenian went slowly out into the passage and shouted: 'Mashya, come and pour out tea! Where are you, Mashya?'

Hurried footsteps were heard, and there came into the room a girl of sixteen in a simple cotton dress and a white kerchief. As she washed the crockery and poured out the tea, she was standing with her back to me, and all I could see was that she was of a slender figure, barefooted, and that her little bare heels were covered by long trousers.

The Armenian invited me to have tea. Sitting down to the table, I glanced at the girl, who was handing me a glass of tea, and felt all at once as though a wind were blowing over my soul and blowing away all the impressions of the day with their dust and dreariness. I saw the bewitching features of the most beautiful face I have ever met in real life or in my dreams. Before me stood a beauty, and I recognised that at the first glance as I should have recognised lightning.

I am ready to swear that Masha – or, as her father called her, Mashya – was a real beauty, but I don't know how to prove it. It sometimes happens that clouds are huddled together in disorder on the horizon, and the sun hiding behind them colours them and the sky with tints of every possible shade – crimson, orange, gold, lilac, muddy pink; one cloud is like a monk, another like a fish, a third like a Turk in a turban. The glow of sunset enveloping a third of the sky gleams on the cross on the church, flashes on the windows of the manor house, is reflected in the river and the puddles, quivers on the trees; far, far away against the background of the sunset, a flock of wild ducks is flying homewards . . . And the boy herding the cows, and the surveyor driving in his chaise over the dam, and the gentleman out for a walk, all gaze at the sunset, and every one of them thinks it terribly beautiful, but no one knows or can say in what its beauty lies.

I was not the only one to think the Armenian girl beautiful. My grandfather, an old man of seventy, gruff and indifferent to women and the beauties of nature, looked caressingly at Masha for a full minute, and asked:

'Is that your daughter, Avert Nazaritch?'

'Yes, she is my daughter,' answered the Armenian.

'A fine young lady,' said my grandfather approvingly.

An artist would have called the Armenian girl's beauty classical and severe, it was just that beauty, the contemplation of which – God knows why! – inspires in one the conviction that one is seeing correct features; that hair, eyes, nose, mouth, neck, bosom, and every movement of the young body all go together in one complete harmonious accord in which nature has not blundered over the smallest line. You fancy for some reason that the ideally beautiful woman must have such a nose as Masha's, straight and slightly aquiline, just such great dark eyes, such long lashes, such a languid glance; you fancy that her black curly hair and eyebrows go with the soft white tint of her brow and cheeks as the green reeds go with the quiet stream. Masha's white neck and her youthful bosom were not fully developed, but you fancy the sculptor would need a great creative genius to mould them. You gaze, and little by little the desire comes over you to say to Masha something extraordinarily pleasant, sincere, beautiful, as beautiful as she herself was.

At first I felt hurt and abashed that Masha took no notice of me, but was all the time looking down; it seemed to me as though a peculiar atmosphere, proud and happy, separated her from me and jealously screened her from my eyes.

'That's because I am covered with dust,' I thought, 'am sunburnt, and am still a boy.'

But little by little I forgot myself, and gave myself up entirely to the consciousness of beauty. I thought no more now of the dreary steppe, of the dust, no longer heard the buzzing of the flies, no longer tasted the tea, and felt nothing except that a beautiful girl was standing only the other side of the table.

I felt this beauty rather strangely. It was not desire, nor ecstasy, nor enjoyment that Masha excited in me, but a painful though pleasant sadness. It was a sadness vague and undefined as a dream. For some reason I felt sorry for myself, for my grandfather and for the Armenian, even for the girl herself, and I had a feeling as though we all four had lost something important and essential to life which we should never find again. My grandfather, too, grew melancholy; he talked no more about manure or about oats, but sat silent, looking pensively at Masha.

After tea my grandfather lay down for a nap while I went out of the house into the porch. The house, like all the houses in the Armenian village stood in the full sun; there was not a tree, not an awning, no shade. The Armenian's great courtyard, overgrown with goosefoot and wild mallows, was lively and full of gaiety in spite of the great heat. Threshing was going on behind one of the low hurdles which intersected the big yard here and there. Round a post stuck into the middle of the threshing-floor ran a dozen horses harnessed side by side, so that they formed one long radius. A Little Russian in a long waistcoat and full trousers was walking beside them, cracking a whip and shouting in a tone that sounded as though he were jeering at the horses and showing off his power over them.

'A – a – a, you damned brutes! . . . A – a – a, plague take you! Are you frightened?'

The horses, sorrel, white, and piebald, not understanding why they were made to run round in one place and to crush the wheat straw, ran unwillingly as though with effort, swinging their tails with an offended air. The wind raised up perfect clouds of golden chaff from under their hoofs and carried it away far beyond the hurdle. Near the tall fresh stacks peasant women were swarming with rakes, and carts were moving, and beyond the stacks in another yard another dozen similar horses were running round a post, and a similar Little Russian was cracking his whip and jeering at the horses.

The steps on which I was sitting were hot; on the thin rails and here and there on the window-frames sap was oozing out of the wood from the heat; red ladybirds were huddling together in the streaks of shadow under the steps and under the shutters. The sun was baking me on my head, on my chest, and on my back, but I did not notice it, and was conscious only of the thud of bare feet on the uneven floor in the passage and in the rooms behind me. After clearing away the tea-things, Masha ran down the steps, fluttering the air as she passed, and like a bird flew into a little grimy outhouse – I suppose the kitchen – from which came the smell of roast mutton and the sound of angry talk in

Armenian. She vanished into the dark doorway, and in her place there appeared on the threshold an old bent, red-faced Armenian woman wearing green trousers. The old woman was angry and was scolding someone. Soon afterwards Masha appeared in the doorway, flushed with the heat of the kitchen and carrying a big black loaf on her shoulder; swaying gracefully under the weight of the bread, she ran across the yard to the threshing-floor, darted over the hurdle, and, wrapt in a cloud of golden chaff, vanished behind the carts. The Little Russian who was driving the horses lowered his whip, sank into silence, and gazed for a minute in the direction of the carts. Then when the Armenian girl darted again by the horses and leaped over the hurdle, he followed her with his eyes, and shouted to the horses in a tone as though he were greatly disappointed:

'Plague take you, unclean devils!'

And all the while I was unceasingly hearing her bare feet, and seeing how she walked across the yard with a grave, preoccupied face. She ran now down the steps, swishing the air about me, now into the kitchen, now to the threshing-floor, now through the gate, and I could hardly turn my head quickly enough to watch her.

And the oftener she fluttered by me with her beauty, the more acute became my sadness. I felt sorry both for her and for myself and for the Little Russian, who mournfully watched her every time she ran through the cloud of chaff to the carts. Whether it was envy of her beauty, or that I was regretting that the girl was not mine, and never would be, or that I was a stranger to her; or whether I vaguely felt that her rare beauty was accidental, unnecessary, and, like everything on earth, of short duration; or whether, perhaps, my sadness was that peculiar feeling which is excited in man by the contemplation of real beauty, God only knows.

The three hours of waiting passed unnoticed. It seemed to me that I had not had time to look properly at Masha when Karpo drove up to the river, bathed the horse, and began to put it in the shafts. The wet horse snorted with pleasure and kicked his hoofs against the shafts. Karpo shouted to it: 'Ba – ack!' My grandfather woke up. Masha opened the creaking gates for us, we got into the chaise and drove out of the yard. We drove in silence as though we were angry with one another.

When, two or three hours later, Rostov and Nahitchevan appeared in the distance, Karpo, who had been silent the whole time, looked round quickly, and said:

'A fine wench, that at the Armenian's.'

And he lashed his horses.

II

Another time, after I had become a student, I was travelling by rail to the south. It was May. At one of the stations, I believe it was between Byelgorod and Harkov, I got out of the tram to walk about the platform.

The shades of evening were already lying on the station garden, on the platform, and on the fields; the station screened off the sunset, but on the topmost clouds of smoke from the engine, which were tinged with rosy light, one could see the sun had not yet quite vanished.

As I walked up and down the platform I noticed that the greater number of the passengers were standing or walking near a second-class compartment, and that they looked as though some celebrated person were in that compartment. Among the curious whom I met near this compartment I saw, however, an artillery officer who had been my fellow-traveller, an intelligent, cordial, and sympathetic fellow – as people mostly are whom we meet on our travels by chance and with whom we are not long acquainted.

'What are you looking at there?' I asked.

He made no answer, but only indicated with his eyes a feminine figure. It was a young girl of seventeen or eighteen, wearing a Russian dress, with her head bare and a little shawl flung carelessly on one shoulder; not a passenger, but I suppose a sister or daughter of the station-master. She was standing near the carriage window, talking to an elderly woman who was in the train. Before I had time to realise what I was seeing, I was suddenly overwhelmed by the feeling I had once experienced in the Armenian village.

The girl was remarkably beautiful, and that was unmistakable to me and to those who were looking at her as I was.

If one is to describe her appearance feature by feature, as the practice is, the only really lovely thing was her thick wavy fair hair, which hung loose with a black ribbon tied round her head; all the other features were either irregular or very ordinary. Either from a peculiar form of coquettishness, or from short-sightedness, her eyes were screwed up, her nose had an undecided tilt, her mouth was small, her profile was feebly and insipidly drawn, her shoulders were narrow and undeveloped for her age – and yet the girl made the impression of being really beautiful, and looking at her, I was able to feel convinced that the Russian face does not need strict regularity in order to be lovely; what is more, that if instead of her turn-up nose the girl had been given a different one, correct and plastically irreproachable like the Armenian girl's, I fancy her face would have lost all its charm from the change.

Standing at the window talking, the girl, shrugging at the evening damp, continually looking round at us, at one moment put her arms akimbo, at the next raised her hands to her head to straighten her hair, talked, laughed, while her face at one moment wore an expression of wonder, the next of horror, and I don't remember a moment when her face and body were at rest. The whole secret and magic of her beauty lay just in these tiny, infinitely elegant movements, in her smile, in the play of her face, in her rapid glances at us, in the combination of the subtle grace of her movements with her youth, her freshness, the purity of her soul that sounded in her laugh and voice, and with the weakness we love so much in children, in birds, in fawns, and in young trees.

It was that butterfly's beauty so in keeping with waltzing, darting about the garden, laughter and gaiety, and incongruous with serious thought, grief, and repose; and it seemed as though a gust of wind blowing over the platform, or a fall of rain, would be enough to wither the fragile body and scatter the capricious beauty like the pollen of a flower.

'So – o! . . .' the officer muttered with a sigh when, after the second bell, we went back to our compartment.

And what that 'So – o' meant I will not undertake to decide.

Perhaps he was sad, and did not want to go away from the beauty and the spring evening into the stuffy train; or perhaps he, like me, was unaccountably sorry for the beauty, for himself, and for me, and for all the passengers, who were listlessly and reluctantly sauntering back to their compartments. As we passed the station window, at which a pale, red-haired telegraphist with upstanding curls and a faded, broad-cheeked face was sitting beside his apparatus, the officer heaved a sigh and said:

'I bet that telegraphist is in love with that pretty girl. To live out in the wilds under one roof with that ethereal creature and not fall in love is beyond the power of man. And what a calamity, my friend! what an ironical fate, to be stooping, unkempt, grey, a decent fellow and not a fool, and to be in love with that pretty, stupid little girl who would never take a scrap of notice of you! Or worse still: imagine that telegraphist is in love, and at the same time married, and that his wife is as stooping, as unkempt, and as decent a person as himself.'

On the platform between our carriage and the next the guard was standing with his elbows on the railing, looking in the direction of the beautiful girl, and his battered, wrinkled, unpleasantly beefy face, exhausted by sleepless nights and the jolting of the train, wore a look of tenderness and of the deepest sadness, as though in that girl he saw happiness, his own youth, soberness, purity, wife, children; as though he were repenting and feeling in his whole being that that girl was not his, and that for him, with his premature old age, his uncouthness, and his beefy face, the ordinary happiness of a man and a passenger was as far away as heaven . . .

The third bell rang, the whistles sounded, and the train slowly moved off. First the guard, the station-master, then the garden, the beautiful girl with her exquisitely sly smile, passed before our windows . . .

Putting my head out and looking back, I saw how, looking after the train, she walked along the platform by the window where the telegraph clerk was sitting, smoothed her hair, and ran into the garden. The station no longer screened off the sunset, the plain lay open before us, but the sun had already set and the smoke lay in black clouds over the green, velvety young corn. It was melancholy in the spring air, and in the darkening sky, and in the railway carriage.

The familiar figure of the guard came into the carriage, and he began lighting the candles.

Alice in Wonderland *(excerpt)*

LEWIS CARROLL

'**O**h, I've had such a curious dream!' said Alice, and she told her sister, as well as she could remember them, all these strange Adventures of hers that you have just been reading about; and when she had finished, her sister kissed her, and said, 'It *was* a curious dream, dear, certainly: but now run in to your tea; it's getting late.' So Alice got up and ran off, thinking while she ran, as well she might, what a wonderful dream it had been.

But her sister sat still just as she left her, leaning her head on her hand, watching the setting sun, and thinking of little Alice and all her wonderful Adventures, till she too began dreaming after a fashion, and this was her dream: –

First, she dreamed of little Alice herself, and once again the tiny hands were clasped upon her knee, and the bright eager eyes were looking up into hers – she could hear the very tones of her voice, and see that queer little toss of her head to keep back the wandering hair that *would* always get into her eyes – and still as she listened, or seemed to listen, the whole place around her became alive with the strange creatures of her little sister's dream.

The long grass rustled at her feet as the White Rabbit hurried by – the frightened Mouse splashed his way through the neighbouring pool – she could hear the rattle of the teacups as the March Hare and his friends shared their never-ending meal, and the shrill voice of the Queen ordering off her unfortunate guests to execution – once more the pig-baby was sneezing on the Duchess's knee, while plates and dishes crashed around it – once more the shriek of the Gryphon, the squeaking of the Lizard's slate-pencil, and the choking of the suppressed guinea-pigs, filled the air, mixed up with the distant sobs of the miserable Mock Turtle.

So she sat on, with closed eyes, and half believed herself in Wonderland, though she knew she had but to open them again, and all would change to dull reality – the grass would be only rustling in the wind, and the pool rippling to the waving of the reeds – the rattling teacups would change to tinkling sheep-bells, and the Queen's shrill cries to the voice of the shepherd boy – and the sneeze of the baby, the shriek of the Gryphon, and all the other queer noises, would change (she knew) to the confused clamour of the busy farm-yard – while the lowing of the cattle in the distance would take the place of the Mock Turtle's heavy sobs.

Lastly, she pictured to herself how this same little sister of hers would, in the after-time, be herself a grown woman; and how she would keep, through all her riper years, the simple and loving heart of her childhood: and how she would gather about her other little children, and make *their* eyes bright and eager with many a strange tale, perhaps even with the dream of Wonderland of long ago: and how she would feel with all their simple sorrows, and find a pleasure in all their simple joys, remembering her own child-life, and the happy summer days.

Kew Gardens

VIRGINIA WOOLF

From the oval-shaped flower-bed there rose perhaps a hundred stalks spreading into heart-shaped or tongue-shaped leaves half way up and unfurling at the tip red or blue or yellow petals marked with spots of colour raised upon the surface; and from the red, blue or yellow gloom of the throat emerged a straight bar, rough with gold dust and slightly clubbed at the end. The petals were voluminous enough to be stirred by the summer breeze, and when they moved, the red, blue and yellow lights passed one over the other, staining an inch of the brown earth beneath with a spot of the most intricate colour. The light fell either upon the smooth, grey back of a pebble, or, the shell of a snail with its brown, circular veins, or falling into a raindrop, it expanded with such intensity of red, blue and yellow the thin walls of water that one expected them to burst and disappear. Instead, the drop was left in a second silver grey once more, and the light now settled upon the flesh of a leaf, revealing the branching thread of fibre beneath the surface, and again it moved on and spread its illumination in the vast green spaces beneath the dome of the heart-shaped and tongue-shaped leaves. Then the breeze stirred rather more briskly overhead and the colour was flashed into the air above, into the eyes of the men and women who walk in Kew Gardens in July.

The figures of these men and women straggled past the flower-bed with a curiously irregular movement not unlike that of the white and blue butterflies who crossed the turf in zig-zag flights from bed to bed. The man was about six inches in front of the woman, strolling carelessly, while she bore on with greater purpose, only turning her head now and then to see that the children were not too far behind. The man kept this distance in front of the woman purposely, though perhaps unconsciously, for he wished to go on with his thoughts.

'Fifteen years ago I came here with Lily,' he thought. 'We sat somewhere over there by a lake and I begged her to marry me all through the hot afternoon. How the dragonfly kept circling round us: how clearly I see the dragonfly and her shoe with the square silver buckle at the toe. All the time I spoke I saw her shoe and when it moved impatiently I knew without looking up what she was going to say: the whole of her seemed to be in her shoe. And my love, my desire, were in the dragonfly; for some reason I thought that if it settled there, on that leaf, the broad one with the red flower in the middle of it, if the dragonfly settled on the leaf she would say 'Yes' at once. But the dragonfly went round and round: it never settled anywhere – of course not, happily not, or I shouldn't be walking here with Eleanor and the children – Tell me, Eleanor. D'you ever think of the past?'

'Why do you ask, Simon?'

'Because I've been thinking of the past. I've been thinking of Lily, the woman I might have married . . . Well, why are you silent? Do you mind my thinking of the past?'

'Why should I mind, Simon? Doesn't one always think of the past, in a garden with men and women lying under the trees? Aren't they one's past, all that remains of it, those men and women, those ghosts lying under the trees . . . one's happiness, one's reality?'

'For me, a square silver shoe buckle and a dragonfly—'

'For me, a kiss. Imagine six little girls sitting before their easels twenty years ago, down by the side of a lake, painting the water-lilies, the first red water-lilies I'd ever seen. And suddenly a kiss, there on the back of my neck. And my hand shook all the afternoon so that I couldn't paint. I took out my watch and marked the hour when I would allow myself to think of the kiss for five minutes only – it was so precious – the kiss of an old grey-haired woman with a wart on her nose, the mother of all my kisses all my life. Come, Caroline, come, Hubert.'

They walked on past the flower-bed, now walking four abreast, and soon diminished in size among the trees and looked half transparent as the sunlight and shade swam over their backs in large trembling irregular patches.

In the oval flower-bed the snail, whose shell had been stained red, blue, and yellow for the space of two minutes or so, now appeared to be moving very slightly in its shell, and next began to labour over the crumbs of loose earth which broke away and rolled down as it passed over them. It appeared to have a defi-nite goal in front of it, differing in this respect from the singular high-stepping angular green insect who attempted to cross in front of it, and waited for a second with its antennæ trembling as if in deliberation, and then stepped off as rapidly and strangely in the opposite direction. Brown cliffs with deep green lakes in the hollows, flat, blade-like trees that waved from root to tip, round boulders of grey stone, vast crumpled surfaces of a thin crackling texture – all these objects lay across the snail's progress between one stalk and another to his goal. Before he had decided whether to circumvent the arched tent of a dead leaf or to breast it there came past the bed the feet of other human beings.

This time they were both men. The younger of the two wore an expression of perhaps unnatural calm; he raised his eyes and fixed them very steadily in front of him while his companion spoke, and directly his companion had done speaking he looked on the ground again and sometimes opened his lips only after a long pause and sometimes did not open them at all. The elder man had a curiously uneven and shaky method of walking, jerking his hand forward and throwing up his head abruptly, rather in the manner of an impatient carriage horse tired of waiting outside a house; but in the man these gestures were irresolute and pointless. He talked almost incessantly; he smiled to himself and again began to talk, as if the smile had been an answer. He was talking about spirits – the spirits of the dead, who, according to him, were even now telling him all sorts of odd things about their experiences in Heaven.

'Heaven was known to the ancients as Thessaly, William, and now, with this war, the spirit matter is rolling between the hills like thunder.' He paused, seemed to listen, smiled, jerked his head and continued: –

'You have a small electric battery and a piece of rubber to insulate the wire – isolate? – insulate? – well, we'll skip the details, no good going into details that wouldn't be understood – and in short the little machine stands in any convenient position by the head of the bed, we will say, on a neat mahogany stand. All arrangements being properly fixed by workmen under my direction, the widow applies her ear and summons the spirit by sign as agreed. Women! Widows! Women in black—'

Here he seemed to have caught sight of a woman's dress in the distance, which in the shade looked a purple black. He took off his hat, placed his hand upon his heart, and hurried towards her muttering and gesticulating feverishly. But William caught him by the sleeve and touched a flower with the tip of his walking-stick in order to divert the old man's attention. After looking at it for a moment in some confusion the old man bent his ear to it and seemed to answer a voice speaking from it, for he began talking about the forests of Uruguay which he had visited hundreds of years ago in company with the most beautiful young woman in Europe. He could be heard murmuring about forests of Uruguay blanketed with the wax petals of tropical roses, nightingales, sea beaches, mermaids, and women drowned at sea, as he suffered himself to be moved on by William, upon whose face the look of stoical patience grew slowly deeper and deeper.

Following his steps so closely as to be slightly puzzled by his gestures came two elderly women of the lower middle class, one stout and ponderous, the other rosy cheeked and nimble. Like most people of their station they were frankly fascinated by any signs of eccentricity betokening a disordered brain, especially in the well-to-do; but they were too far off to be certain whether the gestures were merely eccentric or genuinely mad. After they had scrutinised the old man's back in silence for a moment and given each other a queer, sly look, they went on energetically piecing together their very complicated dialogue:

'Nell, Bert, Lot, Cess, Phil, Pa, he says, I says, she says, I says, I says, I says—'

'My Bert, Sis, Bill, Grandad, the old man, sugar,

Sugar, flour, kippers, greens,

Sugar, sugar, sugar.'

The ponderous woman looked through the pattern of falling words at the flowers standing cool, firm, and upright in the earth, with a curious expression. She saw them as a sleeper waking from a heavy sleep sees a brass candlestick reflecting the light in an unfamiliar way, and closes his eyes and opens them, and seeing the brass candlestick again, finally starts broad awake and stares at the candlestick with all his powers. So the heavy woman came to a standstill opposite the oval-shaped flower-bed, and ceased even to pretend to listen to what the other woman was saying. She stood there letting the words fall over her, swaying the top part of her body slowly backwards and forwards, looking at the flowers. Then she suggested that they should find a seat and have their tea.

The snail had now considered every possible method of reaching his goal without going round the dead leaf or climbing over it. Let alone the effort needed for climbing a leaf, he was doubtful whether the thin texture which vibrated with such an alarming crackle when touched even by the tip of his horns would bear his weight; and this determined him finally to creep beneath it, for there was a point where the leaf curved high enough from the ground to admit him. He had just inserted his head in the opening and was taking stock of the high brown roof and was getting used to the cool brown light when two other people came past outside on the turf. This time they were both young, a young man and a young woman. They were both in the prime of youth, or even in that season which precedes the prime of youth, the season before the smooth pink folds of the flower have burst their gummy case, when the wings of the butterfly, though fully grown, are motionless in the sun.

'Lucky it isn't Friday,' he observed.

'Why? D'you believe in luck?'

'They make you pay sixpence on Friday.'

'What's sixpence anyway? Isn't it worth sixpence?'

'What's "it" – what do you mean by "it"?'

'O, anything – I mean – you know what I mean.'

Long pauses came between each of these remarks; they were uttered in toneless and monotonous voices. The couple stood still on the edge of the flower-bed, and together pressed the end of her parasol deep down into the soft earth. The action and the fact that his hand rested on the top of hers expressed their feelings in a strange way, as these short insignificant words also expressed something, words with short wings for their heavy body of mean-ing, inadequate to carry them far and thus alighting awkwardly upon the very common objects that surrounded them, and were to their inexperienced touch so massive; but who knows (so they thought as they pressed the parasol into the earth) what precipices aren't concealed in them, or what slopes of ice don't shine in the sun on the other side? Who knows? Who has ever seen this before? Even when she wondered what sort of tea they gave you at Kew, he felt that something loomed up behind her words, and stood vast and solid behind them; and the mist very slowly rose and uncovered – O, Heavens, what were those shapes? – little white tables, and waitresses who looked first at her and then at him; and there was a bill that he would pay with a real two-shilling piece, and it was real, all real, he assured himself, fingering the coin in his pocket, real to everyone except to him and to her; even to him it began to seem real; and then – but it was too exciting to stand and think any longer, and he pulled the parasol out of the earth with a jerk and was impatient to find the place where one had tea with other people, like other people.

'Come along, Trissie; it's time we had our tea.'

'Wherever *does* one have one's tea?' she asked with the oddest thrill of excitement in her voice, looking vaguely round and letting herself be drawn on down the grass path, trailing her parasol, turning her head this way and that way, forgetting her tea, wishing to go down there and then down there, remembering orchids and cranes among wild flowers, a Chinese pagoda and a crimson crested bird; but he bore her on.

Thus one couple after another with much the same irregular and aimless movement passed the flower-bed and were enveloped in layer after layer of green blue vapour, in which at first their bodies had substance and a dash of colour, but later both substance and colour dissolved in the green-blue atmosphere. How hot it was! So hot that even the thrush chose to hop, like a mechanical bird, in the shadow of the flowers, with long pauses between one movement and the next; instead of rambling vaguely the white butterflies danced one above another, making with their white shifting flakes the outline of a shattered marble column above the tallest flowers; the glass roofs of the palm house shone as if a whole market full of shiny green umbrellas had opened in the sun; and in the drone of the aeroplane the voice of the summer sky murmured its fierce soul. Yellow and black, pink and snow white, shapes of all these colours, men, women, and children were spotted for a second upon the horizon, and then, seeing the breadth of yellow that lay upon the grass, they wavered and sought shade beneath the trees, dissolving like drops of water in the yellow and green atmosphere, staining it faintly with red and blue. It seemed as if all gross and heavy bodies had sunk down in the heat motionless and lay huddled upon the ground, but their voices went wavering from them as if they were flames lolling from the thick waxen bodies of candles. Voices. Yes, voices. Wordless voices, breaking the silence suddenly with such depth of contentment, such passion of desire, or, in the voices of children, such freshness of surprise; breaking the silence? But there was no silence; all the time the motor omnibuses were turning their wheels and changing their gear; like a vast nest of Chinese boxes all of wrought steel turning ceaselessly one within another the city murmured; on the top of which the voices cried aloud and the petals of myriads of flowers flashed their colours into the air.

The Legend of O'Donoghue

T. CROFTON CROKER

*I*n an age so distant that the precise period is unknown, a
chieftain named O'Donoghue ruled over the country which
surrounds the romantic Lough Lean, now called the lake of
Killarney. Wisdom, beneficence, and justice distinguished his
reign, and the prosperity and happiness of his subjects were their
natural results. He is said to have been as renowned for his
warlike exploits as for his pacific virtues; and as a proof that his
domestic administration was not the less rigorous because it was
mild, a rocky island is pointed out to strangers, called
'O'Donoghue's Prison', in which this prince once confined his
own son for some act of disorder and disobedience.

His end – for it cannot correctly be called his death – was
singular and mysterious. At one of those splendid feasts for which
his court was celebrated, surrounded by the most distinguished
of his subjects, he was engaged in a prophetic relation of the
events which were to happen in ages yet to come. His auditors
listened, now wrapt in wonder, now fired with indignation, burning with shame, or melted into sorrow, as he faithfully detailed

the heroism, the injuries, the crimes, and the miseries of their descendants. In the midst of his predictions he rose slowly from his seat, advanced with a solemn, measured, and majestic tread to the shore of the lake, and walked forward composedly upon its unyielding surface. When he had nearly reached the centre he paused for a moment, then, turning slowly round, looked toward his friends, and waving his arms to them with the cheerful air of one taking a short farewell, disappeared from their view.

The memory of the good O'Donoghue has been cherished by successive generations with affectionate reverence; and it is believed that at sunrise, on every May-day morning, the anniversary of his departure, he revisits his ancient domains: a favoured few only are in general permitted to see him, and this distinction is always an omen of good fortune to the beholders; when it is granted to many it is a sure token of an abundant harvest – a blessing, the want of which during this prince's reign was never felt by his people.

Some years have elapsed since the last appearance of O'Donoghue. The April of that year had been remarkably wild and stormy; but on May-morning the fury of the elements had altogether subsided. The air was hushed and still; and the sky, which was reflected in the serene lake, resembled a beautiful but deceitful countenance, whose smiles, after the most tempestuous emotions, tempt the stranger to believe that it belongs to a soul which no passion has ever ruffled.

The first beams of the rising sun were just gilding the lofty summit of Glenaa, when the waters near the eastern shore of the lake became suddenly and violently agitated, though all the rest of its surface lay smooth and still as a tomb of polished marble, the next morning a foaming wave darted forward, and, like a proud high-crested war-horse, exulting in his strength, rushed across the lake toward Toomies mountain. Behind this wave appeared a stately warrior fully armed, mounted upon a milk-white steed; his snowy plume waved gracefully from a helmet of polished steel, and at his back fluttered a light blue scarf. The horse, apparently exulting in his noble burden, sprung after the wave along the water, which bore him up like firm earth, while showers of spray that glittered brightly in the morning sun were dashed up at every bound.

The warrior was O'Donoghue; he was followed by numberless youths and maidens, who moved lightly and unconstrained over the watery plain, as the moonlight fairies glide through the fields of air; they were linked together by garlands of delicious spring flowers, and they timed their movements to strains of enchanting melody. When O'Donoghue had nearly reached the western side of the lake, he suddenly turned his steed, and directed his course along the wood-fringed shore of Glenaa, preceded by the huge wave that curled and foamed up as high as the horse's neck, whose fiery nostrils snorted above it. The long train of attendants followed with playful deviations the track of their leader, and moved on with unabated fleetness to their celestial music, till gradually, as they entered the narrow strait between Glenaa and Dinis, they became involved in the mists which still partially floated over the lakes, and faded from the view of the wondering beholders: but the sound of their music still fell upon the ear, and echo, catching up the harmonious strains, fondly repeated and prolonged them in soft and softer tones, till the last faint repetition died away, and the hearers awoke as from a dream of bliss.

Wynken, Blynken and Nod

EUGENE FIELD

Wynken, Blynken, and Nod one night
   Sailed off in a wooden shoe, –
Sailed on a river of crystal light
   Into a sea of dew.
'Where are you going, and what do you wish?'
   The old moon asked the three.
'We have come to fish for the herring-fish
   That live in this beautiful sea;
   Nets of silver and gold have we,'
     Said Wynken,
     Blynken,
     And Nod.

The old moon laughed and sang a song,
   As they rocked in the wooden shoe;

And the wind that sped them all night long
 Ruffled the waves of dew;
The little stars were the herring-fish
 That lived in the beautiful sea.
'Now cast your nets wherever you wish, –
 Never afraid are we!'
 So cried the stars to the fishermen three,
 Wynken,
 Blynken,
 And Nod.

All night long their nets they threw
 To the stars in the twinkling foam, –
Then down from the skies came the wooden shoe,
 Bringing the fishermen home:
'Twas all so pretty a sail, it seemed
 As if it could not be;
And some folk thought 'twas a dream they'd
 dreamed
 Of sailing that beautiful sea;
 But I shall name you the fishermen three:
 Wynken,
 Blynken,
 And Nod.

Wynken and Blynken are two little eyes,
    And Nod is a little head,
And the wooden shoe that sailed the skies
    Is a wee one's trundle-bed;
So shut your eyes while Mother sings
    Of wonderful sights that be,
And you shall see the beautiful things
    As you rock in the misty sea
    Where the old shoe rocked the fishermen three: –
    Wynken,
    Blynken,
    And Nod.

Xingu

EDITH WHARTON

I

Mrs Ballinger is one of the ladies who pursue Culture in bands, as though it were dangerous to meet alone. To this end she had founded the Lunch Club, an association composed of herself and several other indomitable huntresses of erudition. The Lunch Club, after three or four winters of lunching and debate, had acquired such local distinction that the entertainment of distinguished strangers became one of its accepted functions; in recognition of which it duly extended to the celebrated 'Osric Dane', on the day of her arrival in Hillbridge, an invitation to be present at the next meeting.

The club was to meet at Mrs Ballinger's. The other members, behind her back, were of one voice in deploring her unwillingness to cede her rights in favour of Mrs Plinth, whose house made a more impressive setting for the entertainment of celebrities; while, as Mrs Leveret observed, there was always the picture-gallery to fall back on.

Mrs Plinth made no secret of sharing this view. She had always regarded it as one of her obligations to entertain the Lunch Club's distinguished guests. Mrs Plinth was almost as proud of her obligations as she was of her picture-gallery; she was in fact fond of implying that the one possession implied the other, and that only a woman of her wealth could afford to live up to a standard as high as that which she had set herself. An all-round sense of duty, roughly adaptable to various ends, was, in her opinion, all that Providence exacted of the more humbly stationed; but the power which had predestined Mrs Plinth to keep a footman clearly intended her to maintain an equally specialised staff of responsibilities. It was the more to be regretted that Mrs Ballinger, whose obligations to society were bounded by the narrow scope of two parlour-maids, should have been so tenacious of the right to entertain Osric Dane.

The question of that lady's reception had for a month past profoundly moved the members of the Lunch Club. It was not that they felt themselves unequal to the task, but that their sense of the opportunity plunged them into the agreeable uncertainty of the lady who weighs the alternatives of a well-stocked wardrobe. If such subsidiary members as Mrs Leveret were fluttered by the thought of exchanging ideas with the author of *The Wings of Death*, no forebodings disturbed the conscious adequacy of Mrs Plinth, Mrs Ballinger and Miss Van Vluyck. *The Wings of Death* had, in fact, at Miss Van Vluyck's suggestion, been chosen as the subject of discussion at the last club meeting, and each member had thus been enabled to express her own opinion or to appropriate whatever sounded well in the comments of the others.

Mrs Roby alone had abstained from profiting by the opportunity; but it was now openly recognised that, as a member of the Lunch Club, Mrs Roby was a failure. 'It all comes,' as Miss Van Vluyck put it, 'of accepting a woman on a man's estimation.' Mrs Roby, returning to Hillbridge from a prolonged sojourn in exotic lands – the other ladies no longer took the trouble to remember where – had been heralded by the distinguished biologist, Professor Foreland, as the most agreeable woman he had ever met; and the members of the Lunch Club, impressed by an encomium that carried the weight of a diploma, and rashly assuming that the Professor's social sympathies would follow the line of his professional bent, had seized the chance of annexing a biological member. Their disillusionment was complete. At Miss Van Vluyck's first off-hand mention of the pterodactyl Mrs Roby had confusedly murmured: 'I know so little about metres—' and after that painful betrayal of incompetence she had prudently withdrawn from farther participation in the mental gymnastics of the club.

'I suppose she flattered him,' Miss Van Vluyck summed up – 'or else it's the way she does her hair.'

The dimensions of Miss Van Vluyck's dining-room having restricted the membership of the club to six, the nonconductiveness of one member was a serious obstacle to the exchange of ideas, and some wonder had already been expressed that Mrs Roby should care to live, as it were, on the intellectual bounty of the others. This feeling was increased by the discovery that she had not yet read *The Wings of Death*. She owned to having heard the name of Osric Dane; but that – incredible as it appeared – was the extent of her acquaintance with the celebrated novelist. The ladies could not conceal their surprise; but Mrs Ballinger, whose pride in the club made her wish to put even Mrs Roby in the best possible light, gently insinuated that, though she had not had time to acquaint herself with *The Wings of Death*, she must at least be familiar with its equally remarkable predecessor, *The Supreme Instant*.

Mrs Roby wrinkled her sunny brows in a conscientious effort of memory, as a result of which she recalled that, oh, yes, she *had* seen the book at her brother's, when she was staying with him in Brazil, and had even carried it off to read one day on a boating party; but they had all got to shying things at each other in the boat, and the book had gone overboard, so she had never had the chance—

The picture evoked by this anecdote did not increase Mrs Roby's credit with the club, and there was a painful pause, which was broken by Mrs Plinth's remarking:

'I can understand that, with all your other pursuits, you should not find much time for reading; but I should have thought you might at least have *got up The Wings of Death* before Osric Dane's arrival.'

Mrs Roby took this rebuke good-humouredly. She had meant, she owned, to glance through the book; but she had been so absorbed in a novel of Trollope's that—

'No one reads Trollope now,' Mrs Ballinger interrupted.

Mrs Roby looked pained. 'I'm only just beginning,' she confessed.

'And does he interest you?' Mrs Plinth enquired.

'He amuses me.'

'Amusement,' said Mrs Plinth, 'is hardly what I look for in my choice of books.'

'Oh, certainly, *The Wings of Death* is not amusing,' ventured Mrs Leveret, whose manner of putting forth an opinion was like that of an obliging salesman with a variety of other styles to submit if his first selection does not suit.

'Was it *meant* to be?' enquired Mrs Plinth, who was fond of asking questions that she permitted no one but herself to answer. 'Assuredly not.'

'Assuredly not – that is what I was going to say,' assented Mrs Leveret, hastily rolling up her opinion and reaching for another. 'It was meant to – to elevate.'

Miss Van Vluyck adjusted her spectacles as though they were the black cap of condemnation. 'I hardly see,' she interposed, 'how a book steeped in the bitterest pessimism can be said to elevate however much it may instruct.'

'I meant, of course, to instruct,' said Mrs Leveret, flurried by the unexpected distinction between two terms which she had supposed to be synonymous. Mrs Leveret's enjoyment of the Lunch Club was frequently marred by such surprises; and not knowing her own value to the other ladies as a mirror for their mental complacency she was sometimes troubled by a doubt of her worthiness to join in their debates. It was only the fact of having a dull sister who thought her clever that saved her, from a sense of hopeless inferiority.

'Do they get married in the end?' Mrs Roby interposed.

'They – who?' the Lunch Club collectively exclaimed.

'Why, the girl and man. It's a novel, isn't it? I always think that's the one thing that matters. If they're parted it spoils my dinner.'

Mrs Plinth and Mrs Ballinger exchanged scandalised glances, and the latter said: 'I should hardly advise you to read *The Wings of Death* in that spirit. For my part, when there are so many books one *has* to read; I wonder how anyone can find time for those that are merely amusing.'

'The beautiful part of it,' Laura Glyde murmured, 'is surely just this – that no one can tell how *The Wings of Death* ends. Osric Dane, overcome by the awful significance of her own meaning, has mercifully veiled it – perhaps even from herself – as Apelles, in representing the sacrifice of Iphigenia, veiled the face of Agamemnon.'

'What's that? Is it poetry?' whispered Mrs Leveret to Mrs Plinth, who, disdaining a definite reply, said coldly: 'You should look it up. I always make it a point to look things up.' Her tone added – 'though I might easily have it done for me by the footman.'

'I was about to say,' Miss Van Vluyck resumed, 'that it must always be a question whether a book *can* instruct unless it elevates.'

'Oh—' murmured Mrs Leveret, now feeling herself hopelessly astray.

'I don't know,' said Mrs Ballinger, scenting in Miss Van Vluyck's tone a tendency to depreciate the coveted distinction of entertaining Osric Dane; 'I don't know that such a question can seriously be raised as to a book which has attracted more atten-tion among thoughtful people than any novel since *Robert Elsmere.*'

'Oh, but don't you see,' exclaimed Laura Glyde, 'that it's just the dark hopelessness of it all – the wonderful tone-scheme of black on black – that makes it such an artistic achievement? It reminded me when I read it of Prince Rupert's *manière noire* . . . the book is etched, not painted, yet one feels the colour-values so intensely . . .'

'Who is he?' Mrs Leveret whispered to her neighbour. 'Someone she's met abroad?'

'The wonderful part of the book,' Mrs Ballinger conceded, 'is that it may be looked at from so many points of view. I hear that as a study of determinism Professor Lupton ranks it with *The Data of Ethics.*'

'I'm told that Osric Dane spent ten years in preparatory stud-ies before beginning to write it,' said Mrs Plinth. 'She looks up everything – verifies everything. It has always been my principle, as you know. Nothing would induce me, now, to put aside a book before I'd finished it, just because I can buy as many more as I want.'

'And what do *you* think of *The Wings of Death?*' Mrs Roby abruptly asked her.

It was the kind of question that might be termed out of order, and the ladies glanced at each other as though disclaiming any share in such a breach of discipline. They all knew there was nothing Mrs Plinth so much disliked as being asked her opinion of a book. Books were written to read; if one read them what more could be expected? To be questioned in detail regarding the contents of a volume seemed to her as great an outrage as being searched for smuggled laces at the Custom House. The club had always respected this idiosyncrasy of Mrs Plinth's. Such opinions as she had were imposing and substantial: her mind, like her house, was furnished with monumental 'pieces' that were not meant to be disarranged; and it was one of the unwritten rules of the Lunch Club that, within her own province, each member's habits of thought should be respected. The meeting therefore closed with an increased sense, on the part of the other ladies, of Mrs Roby's hopeless unfitness to be one of them.

II

Mrs Leveret, on the eventful day, arrived early at Mrs Ballinger's, her volume of *Appropriate Allusions* in her pocket.

It always flustered Mrs Leveret to be late at the Lunch Club: she liked to collect her thoughts and gather a hint, as the others assembled, of the turn the conversation was likely to take. To-day, however, she felt herself completely at a loss; and even the familiar contact of *Appropriate Allusions*, which stuck into her as she sat down, failed to give her any reassurance. It was an admirable little volume, compiled to meet all the social emergencies; so that, whether on the occasion of Anniversaries, joyful or melancholy (as the classification ran), of Banquets, social or municipal, or of Baptisms, Church of England or sectarian, its student need never be at a loss for a pertinent reference. Mrs

Leveret, though she had for years devoutly conned its pages, valued it, however, rather for its moral support than for its practical services; for though in the privacy of her own room she commanded an army of quotations, these invariably deserted her at the critical moment, and the only phrase she retained – *Canst thou draw out leviathan with a hook?* – was one she had never yet found occasion to apply.

To-day she felt that even the complete mastery of the volume would hardly have insured her self-possession; for she thought it probable that, even if she *did*, in some miraculous way, remember an Allusion, it would be only to find that Osric Dane used a different volume (Mrs Leveret was convinced that literary people always carried them), and would consequently not recognise her quotations.

Mrs Leveret's sense of being adrift was intensified by the appearance of Mrs Ballinger's drawing-room. To a careless eye its aspect was unchanged; but those acquainted with Mrs Ballinger's way of arranging her books would instantly have detected the marks of recent perturbation. Mrs Ballinger's province, as a member of the Lunch Club, was the Book of the Day. On that, whatever it was, from a novel to a treatise on experimental psychology, she was confidently, authoritatively 'up'. What became of last year's books, or last week's even; what she did with the 'subjects' she had previously professed with equal authority; no one had ever yet discovered. 'Her mind was an hotel where facts came and went like transient lodgers, without leaving their address behind, and frequently without paying for their board. It was Mrs Ballinger's boast that she was 'abreast with the Thought of the Day', and her pride that this advanced position should be expressed by the books on her table. These volumes, frequently renewed, and almost always damp from the press, bore names generally unfamiliar to Mrs Leveret, and giving her, as she furtively scanned them, a disheartening glimpse of new fields of knowledge to be breathlessly traversed in Mrs Ballinger's wake. But to-day a number of maturer-looking volumes were adroitly mingled with the *primeurs* of the press – Karl Marx jostled Professor Bergson, and the *Confessions of St Augustine* lay beside the last work on 'Mendelism'; so that even to Mrs Leveret's fluttered perceptions it was clear that Mrs Ballinger didn't in the least know what Osric Dane was likely to talk about, and had taken measures to be prepared for anything. Mrs Leveret felt like a passenger on an ocean steamer who is told that there is no immediate danger, but that she had better put on her life-belt.

It was a relief to be roused from these forebodings by Miss Van Vluyck's arrival.

'Well, my dear,' the new-comer briskly asked her hostess, 'what subjects are we to discuss to-day?'

Mrs Ballinger was furtively replacing a volume of Wordsworth by a copy of Verlaine. 'I hardly know,' she said, somewhat nervously. 'Perhaps we had better leave that to circumstances.'

'Circumstances?' said Miss Van Vluyck drily. 'That means, I suppose, that Laura Glyde will take the floor as usual, and we shall be deluged with literature.'

Philanthropy and statistics were Miss Van Vluyck's province, and she resented any tendency to divert their guest's attention from these topics.

Mrs Plinth at this moment appeared.

'Literature?' she protested in a tone of remonstrance. 'But this is perfectly unexpected. I understood we were to talk of Osric Dane's novel.'

Mrs Ballinger winced at the discrimination, but let it pass. 'We can hardly make that our chief subject – at least not *too* intentionally,' she suggested. 'Of course we can let our talk *drift* in that direction; but we ought to have some other topic as an introduction, and that is what I wanted to consult you about. The fact is, we know so little of Osric Dane's tastes and interests that it is difficult to make any special preparation.'

'It may be difficult,' said Mrs Plinth with decision, 'but it is necessary. I know what that happy-go-lucky principle leads to. As I told one of my nieces the other day, there are certain emergencies for which a lady should always be prepared. It's in shocking taste to wear colours when one pays a visit of condolence, or a last year's dress when there are reports that one's husband is on the wrong side of the market; and so it is with conversation. All I ask is that I should know beforehand what is to be talked about; then I feel sure of being able to say the proper thing.'

'I quite agree with you,' Mrs Ballinger assented; 'but—'

And at that instant, heralded by the fluttered parlour-maid, Osric Dane appeared upon the threshold.

Mrs Leveret told her sister afterward that she had known at a glance what was coming. She saw that Osric Dane was not going to meet them half way. That distinguished personage had indeed entered with an air of compulsion not calculated to promote the easy exercise of hospitality. She looked as though she were about to be photographed for a new edition of her books.

The desire to propitiate a divinity is generally in inverse ratio to its responsiveness, and the sense of discouragement produced by Osric Dane's entrance visibly increased the Lunch Club's eagerness to please her. Any lingering idea that she might consider herself under an obligation to her entertainers was at once dispelled by her manner: as Mrs Leveret said afterward to her sister, she had a way of looking at you that made you feel as if there was something wrong with your hat. This evidence of greatness produced such an immediate impression on the ladies that a shudder of awe ran through them when Mrs Roby, as their hostess led the great personage into the dining-room, turned back to whisper to the others: 'What a brute she is!'

The hour about the table did not tend to revise this verdict. It was passed by Osric Dane in the silent deglutition of Mrs Ballinger's menu, and by the members of the club in the emission of tentative platitudes which their guest seemed to swallow as perfunctorily as the successive courses of the luncheon.

Mrs Ballinger's reluctance to fix a topic had thrown the club into a mental disarray which increased with the return to the drawing-room, where the actual business of discussion was to open. Each lady waited for the other to speak; and there was a general shock of disappointment when their hostess opened the conversation by the painfully commonplace enquiry. 'Is this your first visit to Hillbridge?'

Even Mrs Leveret was conscious that this was a bad beginning; and a vague impulse of deprecation made Miss Glyde interject: 'It is a very small place indeed.'

Mrs Plinth bristled. 'We have a great many representative people,' she said, in the tone of one who speaks for her order.

Osric Dane turned to her. 'What do they represent?' she asked.

Mrs Plinth's constitutional dislike to being questioned was intensified by her sense of unpreparedness; and her reproachful glance passed the question on to Mrs Ballinger.

'Why,' said that lady, glancing in turn at the other members, 'as a community I hope it is not too much to say that we stand for culture.'

'For art—' Miss Glyde interjected.

'For art and literature,' Mrs Ballinger emended.

'And for sociology, I trust,' snapped Miss Van Vluyck.

'We have a standard,' said Mrs Plinth, feeling herself suddenly secure on the vast expanse of a generalisation; and Mrs Leveret, thinking there must be room for more than one on so broad a statement, took courage to murmur: 'Oh, certainly; we have a standard.'

'The object of our little club,' Mrs Ballinger continued, 'is to concentrate the highest tendencies of Hillbridge – to centralise and focus its intellectual effort.'

This was felt to be so happy that the ladies drew an almost audible breath of relief.

'We aspire,' the President went on, 'to be in touch with whatever is highest in art, literature and ethics.'

Osric Dane again turned to her. 'What ethics?' she asked.

A tremor of apprehension encircled the room. None of the ladies required any preparation to pronounce on a question of morals; but when they were called ethics it was different. The club, when fresh from the *Encyclopaedia Britannica*, the *Reader's Handbook* or Smith's *Classical Dictionary*, could deal confidently with any subject; but when taken unawares it had been known to define agnosticism as a heresy of the Early Church and Professor Froude as a distinguished histologist; and such minor members as Mrs Leveret still secretly regarded ethics as something vaguely pagan.

Even to Mrs Ballinger, Osric Dane's question was unsettling, and there was a general sense of gratitude when Laura Glyde leaned forward to say, with her most sympathetic accent: 'You must excuse us, Mrs Dane, for not being able, just at present, to talk of anything but *The Wings of Death*.'

'Yes,' said Miss Van Vluyck, with a sudden resolve to carry the war into the enemy's camp. 'We are so anxious to know the exact purpose you had in mind in writing your wonderful book.'

'You will find,' Mrs Plinth interposed, 'that we are not superficial readers.'

'We are eager to hear from you,' Miss Van Vluyck continued, 'if the pessimistic tendency of the book is an expression of your own convictions or—'

'Or merely,' Miss Glyde thrust in, 'a sombre background brushed in to throw your figures into more vivid relief. *Are* you not primarily plastic?'

'I have always maintained,' Mrs Ballinger interposed, 'that you represent the purely objective method—'

Osric Dane helped herself critically to coffee. 'How do you define objective?' she then enquired.

There was a flurried pause before Laura Glyde intensely murmured: 'In reading *you* we don't define, we feel.'

Osric Dane smiled. 'The cerebellum,' she remarked, 'is not infrequently the seat of the literary emotions.' And she took a second lump of sugar.

The sting that this remark was vaguely felt to conceal was almost neutralised by the satisfaction of being addressed in such technical language.

'Ah, the cerebellum,' said Miss Van Vluyck complacently. 'The club took a course in psychology last winter.'

'Which psychology?' asked Osric Dane.

There was an agonising pause, during which each member of the club secretly deplored the distressing inefficiency of the others. Only Mrs Roby went on placidly sipping her chartreuse. At last Mrs Ballinger said, with an attempt at a high tone: 'Well, really, you know, it was last year that we took psychology, and this winter we have been so absorbed in—'

She broke off, nervously trying to recall some of the club's discussions; but her faculties seemed to be paralysed by the petrifying stare of Osric Dane. What *had* the club been absorbed in? Mrs Ballinger, with a vague purpose of gaining time, repeated slowly: 'We've been so intensely absorbed in—'

Mrs Roby put down her liqueur glass and drew near the group with a smile.

'In Xingu?' she gently prompted.

A thrill ran through the other members. They exchanged confused glances, and then, with one accord, turned a gaze of mingled relief and interrogation on their rescuer. The expression of each denoted a different phase of the same emotion. Mrs Plinth was the first to compose her features to an air of reassurance: after a moment's hasty adjustment her look almost implied that it was she who had given the word to Mrs Ballinger.

'Xingu, of course!' exclaimed the latter with her accustomed promptness, while Miss Van Vluyck and Laura Glyde seemed to be plumbing the depths of memory, and Mrs Leveret, feeling apprehensively for *Appropriate Allusions*, was somehow reassured by the uncomfortable pressure of its bulk against her person.

Osric Dane's change of countenance was no less striking than that of her entertainers. She too put down her coffee-cup, but with a look of distinct annoyance; she too wore, for a brief moment, what Mrs Roby afterward described as the look of feeling for something in the back of her head; and before she could dissemble these momentary signs of weakness, Mrs Roby, turning to her with a deferential smile, had said: 'And we've been so hoping that to-day you would tell us just what you think of it.'

Osric Dane received the homage of the smile as a matter of course; but the accompanying question obviously embarrassed her, and it became clear to her observers that she was not quick at shifting her facial scenery. It was as though her countenance had so long been set in an expression of unchallenged superiority that the muscles had stiffened, and refused to obey her orders.

'Xingu—' she said, as if seeking in her turn to gain time.

Mrs Roby continued to press her. 'Knowing how engrossing the subject is, you will understand how it happens that the club has let everything else go to the wall for the moment. Since we took up Xingu I might almost say – were it not for your books – that nothing else seems to us worth remembering.'

Osric Dane's stern features were darkened rather than lit up by an uneasy smile. 'I am glad to hear that you make one exception,' she gave out between narrowed lips.

'Oh, of course,' Mrs Roby said prettily; 'but as you have shown us that – so very naturally! – you don't care to talk of your own things, we really can't let you off from telling us exactly what you think about Xingu; especially,' she added, with a still more persuasive smile, 'as some people say that one of your last books was saturated with it.'

It was an *it*, then – the assurance sped like fire through the parched minds of the other members. In their eagerness to gain the least little clue to Xingu they almost forgot the joy of assisting at the discomfiture of Mrs Dane.

The latter reddened nervously under her antagonist's challenge. 'May I ask,' she faltered out, 'to which of my books you refer?'

Mrs Roby did not falter. 'That's just what I want you to tell us; because, though I was present, I didn't actually take part.'

'Present at what?' Mrs Dane took her up; and for an instant the trembling members of the Lunch Club thought that the champion Providence had raised up for them had lost a point. But Mrs Roby explained herself gaily: 'At the discussion, of course. And so we're dreadfully anxious to know just how it was that you went into the Xingu.'

There was a portentous pause, a silence so big with incalculable dangers that the members with one accord checked the words on their lips, like soldiers dropping their arms to watch a single combat between their leaders. Then Mrs Dane gave expression to their inmost dread by saying sharply: 'Ah – you say *the* Xingu, do you?'

Mrs Roby smiled undauntedly. 'It is a shade pedantic, isn't it? Personally, I always drop the article; but I don't know how the other members feel about it.'

The other members looked as though they would willingly have dispensed with this appeal to their opinion, and Mrs Roby, after a bright glance about the group, went on: 'They probably think, as I do, that nothing really matters except the thing itself – except Xingu.'

No immediate reply seemed to occur to Mrs Dane, and Mrs Ballinger gathered courage to say: 'Surely everyone must feel that about Xingu.'

Mrs Plinth came to her support with a heavy murmur of assent, and Laura Glyde sighed out emotionally: 'I have known cases where it has changed a whole life.'

'It has done me worlds of good,' Mrs Leveret interjected, seeming to herself to remember that she had either taken it or read it the winter before.

'Of course,' Mrs Roby admitted, 'the difficulty is that one must give up so much time to it. It's very long.'

'I can't imagine,' said Miss Van Vluyck, 'grudging the time given to such a subject.'

'And deep in places,' Mrs Roby pursued; (so then it was a book!) 'And it isn't easy to skip.'

'I never skip,' said Mrs Plinth dogmatically.

'Ah, it's dangerous to, in Xingu. Even at the start there are places where one can't. One must just wade through.'

'I should hardly call it *wading*,' said Mrs Ballinger sarcastically.

Mrs Roby sent her a look of interest. 'Ah – you always found it went swimmingly?'

Mrs Ballinger hesitated. 'Of course there are difficult passages,' she conceded.

'Yes; some are not at all clear – even,' Mrs Roby added, 'if one is familiar with the original.'

'As I suppose you are?' Osric Dane interposed, suddenly fixing her with a look of challenge.

Mrs Roby met it by a deprecating gesture. 'Oh, it's really not difficult up to a certain point; though some of the branches are very little known, and it's almost impossible to get at the source.'

'Have you ever tried?' Mrs Plinth enquired, still distrustful of Mrs Roby's thoroughness.

Mrs Roby was silent for a moment; then she replied with lowered lids: 'No – but a friend of mine did; a very brilliant man; and he told me it was best for women – not to . . .'

A shudder ran around the room. Mrs Leveret coughed so that the parlour-maid, who was handing the cigarettes, should not hear; Miss Van Vluyck's face took on a nauseated expression, and Mrs Plinth looked as if she were passing someone she did not care to bow to. But the most remarkable result of Mrs Roby's words was the effect they produced on the Lunch Club's distinguished guest. Osric Dane's impassive features suddenly softened to an expression of the warmest human sympathy, and edging her chair toward Mrs Roby's she asked: 'Did he really? And – did you find he was right?'

Mrs Ballinger, in whom annoyance at Mrs Roby's unwonted assumption of prominence was beginning to displace gratitude for the aid she had rendered, could not consent to her being allowed, by such dubious means, to monopolise the attention of their guest. If Osric Dane had not enough self-respect to resent Mrs Roby's flippancy, at least the Lunch Club would do so in the person of its President.

Mrs Ballinger laid her hand on Mrs Roby's arm. 'We must not forget,' she said with a frigid amiability, 'that absorbing as Xingu is to *us*, it may be less interesting to—'

'Oh, no, on the contrary, I assure you,' Osric Dane intervened.

'—to others,' Mrs Ballinger finished firmly; 'and we must not allow our little meeting to end without persuading Mrs Dane to say a few words to us on a subject which, to-day, is much more present in all our thoughts. I refer, of course, to *The Wings of Death*.'

The other members, animated by various degrees of the same sentiment, and encouraged by the humanised mien of their redoubtable guest, repeated after Mrs Ballinger: 'Oh, yes, you really *must* talk to us a little about your book.'

Osric Dane's expression became as bored, though not as haughty, as when her work had been previously mentioned. But before she could respond to Mrs Ballinger's request, Mrs Roby had risen from her seat, and was pulling down her veil over her frivolous nose.

'I'm so sorry,' she said, advancing toward her hostess with outstretched hand, 'but before Mrs Dane begins I think I'd better run away. Unluckily, as you know, I haven't read her books, so I should be at a terrible disadvantage among you all, and besides, I've an engagement to play bridge.'

If Mrs Roby had simply pleaded her ignorance of Osric Dane's works as a reason for withdrawing, the Lunch Club, in view of her recent prowess, might have approved such evidence of discretion; but to couple this excuse with the brazen announcement that she was foregoing the privilege for the purpose of joining a bridge-party was only one more instance of her deplorable lack of discrimination.

The ladies were disposed, however, to feel that her departure – now that she had performed the sole service she was ever likely to render them – would probably make for greater order and dignity in the impending discussion, besides relieving them of the sense of self-distrust which her presence always mysteriously produced. Mrs Ballinger therefore restricted herself to a formal murmur of regret, and the other members were just grouping themselves comfortably about Osric Dane when the latter, to their dismay, started up from the sofa on which she had been seated.

'Oh wait – do wait, and I'll go with you!' she called out to Mrs Roby; and, seizing the hands of the disconcerted members, she administered a series of farewell pressures with the mechanical haste of a railway-conductor punching tickets.

'I'm so sorry – I'd quite forgotten—' she flung back at them from the threshold; and as she joined Mrs Roby, who had turned in surprise at her appeal, the other ladies had the mortification of hearing her say, in a voice which she did not take the pains to lower: 'If you'll let me walk a little way with you, I should so like to ask you a few more questions about Xingu . . .'

III

The incident had been so rapid that the door closed on the departing pair before the other members had time to understand what was happening. Then a sense of the indignity put upon them by Osric Dane's unceremonious desertion began to contend with the confused feeling that they had been cheated out of their due without exactly knowing how or why.

There was a silence, during which Mrs Ballinger, with a perfunctory hand, rearranged the skilfully grouped literature at which her distinguished guest had not so much as glanced; then Miss Van Vluyck tartly pronounced: 'Well, I can't say that I consider Osric Dane's departure a great loss.'

This confession crystallised the resentment of the other members, and Mrs Leveret exclaimed: 'I do believe she came on purpose to be nasty!'

It was Mrs Plinth's private opinion that Osric Dane's attitude toward the Lunch Club might have been very different had it welcomed her in the majestic setting of the Plinth drawing-rooms; but not liking to reflect on the inadequacy of Mrs

Ballinger's establishment she sought a roundabout satisfaction in depreciating her lack of foresight.

'I said from the first that we ought to have had a subject ready. It's what always happens when you're unprepared. Now if we'd only got up Xingu—'

The slowness of Mrs Plinth's mental processes was always allowed for by the club; but this instance of it was too much for Mrs Ballinger's equanimity.

'Xingu!' she scoffed. 'Why, it was the fact of our knowing so much more about it than she did – unprepared though we were – that made Osric Dane so furious. I should have thought that was plain enough to everybody!'

This retort impressed even Mrs Plinth, and Laura Glyde, moved by an impulse of generosity, said: 'Yes, we really ought to be grateful to Mrs Roby for introducing the topic. It may have made Osric Dane furious, but at least it made her civil.'

'I am glad we were able to show her,' added Miss Van Vluyck, 'that a broad and up-to-date culture is not confined to the great intellectual centres.'

This increased the satisfaction of the other members, and they began to forget their wrath against Osric Dane in the pleasure of having contributed to her discomfiture.

Miss Van Vluyck thoughtfully rubbed her spectacles. 'What surprised me most,' she continued, 'was that Fanny Roby should be so up on Xingu.'

This remark threw a slight chill on the company, but Mrs Ballinger said with an air of indulgent irony: 'Mrs Roby always has the knack of making a little go a long way; still, we certainly owe her a debt for happening to remember that she'd heard of Xingu.' And this was felt by the other members to be a graceful way of cancelling once for all the club's obligation to Mrs Roby.

Even Mrs Leveret took courage to speed a timid shaft of irony. 'I fancy Osric Dane hardly expected to take a lesson in Xingu at Hillbridge!'

Mrs Ballinger smiled. 'When she asked me what we represented – do you remember? – I wish I'd simply said we represented Xingu!'

All the ladies laughed appreciatively at this sally, except Mrs Plinth, who said, after a moment's deliberation: 'I'm not sure it would have been wise to do so.'

Mrs Ballinger, who was already beginning to feel as if she had launched at Osric Dane the retort which had just occurred to her, turned ironically on Mrs Plinth. 'May I ask why?' she enquired.

Mrs Plinth looked grave. 'Surely,' she said, 'I understood from Mrs Roby herself that the subject was one it was as well not to go into too deeply?'

Miss Van Vluyck rejoined with precision: 'I think that applied only to an investigation of the origin of the – of the—'; and suddenly she found that her usually accurate memory had failed her. 'It's a part of the subject I never studied myself,' she concluded.

'Nor I,' said Mrs Ballinger.

Laura Glyde bent toward them with widened eyes. 'And yet it seems – doesn't it? – the part that is fullest of an esoteric fascination?'

'I don't know on what you base that,' said Miss Van Vluyck argumentatively.

'Well, didn't you notice how intensely interested Osric Dane became as soon as she heard what the brilliant foreigner – he *was* a foreigner, wasn't he? – had told Mrs Roby about the origin – the origin of the rite – or whatever you call it?'

Mrs Plinth looked disapproving, and Mrs Ballinger visibly wavered. Then she said: 'It may not be desirable to touch on the – on that part of the subject in general conversation; but, from the importance it evidently has to a woman of Osric Dane's distinction, I feel as if we ought not to be afraid to discuss it among ourselves – without gloves – though with closed doors, if necessary.'

'I'm quite of your opinion,' Miss Van Vluyck came briskly to her support; 'on condition, that is, that all grossness of language is avoided.'

'Oh, I'm sure we shall understand without that,' Mrs Leveret tittered; and Laura Glyde added significantly: 'I fancy we can read between the lines,' while Mrs Ballinger rose to assure herself that the doors were really closed.

Mrs Plinth had not yet given her adhesion. 'I hardly see,' she began, 'what benefit is to be derived from investigating such peculiar customs—'

But Mrs Ballinger's patience had reached the extreme limit of tension. 'This at least,' she returned; 'that we shall not be placed again in the humiliating position of finding ourselves less up on our own subjects than Fanny Roby!'

Even to Mrs Plinth this argument was conclusive. She peered furtively about the room and lowered her commanding tones to ask: 'Have you got a copy?'

'A – a copy?' stammered Mrs Ballinger. She was aware that the other members were looking at her expectantly, and that this answer was inadequate, so she supported it by asking another question. 'A copy of what?'

Her companions bent their expectant gaze on Mrs Plinth, who, in turn, appeared less sure of herself than usual. 'Why, of – of – the book,' she explained.

'What book?' snapped Miss Van Vluyck, almost as sharply as Osric Dane.

Mrs Ballinger looked at Laura Glyde, whose eyes were interrogatively fixed on Mrs Leveret. The fact of being deferred to was so new to the latter that it filled her with an insane temerity. 'Why, Xingu, of course!' she exclaimed.

A profound silence followed this challenge to the resources of Mrs Ballinger's library, and the latter, after glancing nervously toward the Books of the Day, returned with dignity: 'It's not a thing one cares to leave about.'

'I should think not!' exclaimed Mrs Plinth.

'It *is* a book, then?' said Miss Van Vluyck.

This again threw the company into disarray, and Mrs Ballinger, with an impatient sigh, rejoined: 'Why – there *is* a book – naturally . . .'

'Then why did Miss Glyde call it a religion?'

Laura Glyde started up. 'A religion? I never—'

'Yes, you did,' Miss Van Vluyck insisted; 'you spoke of rites; and Mrs Plinth said it was a custom.'

Miss Glyde was evidently making a desperate effort to recall her statement; but accuracy of detail was not her strongest point.

At length she began in a deep murmur: 'Surely they used to do something of the kind at the Eleusinian mysteries—'

'Oh—' said Miss Van Vluyck, on the verge of disapproval; and Mrs Plinth protested: 'I understood there was to be no indelicacy!'

Mrs Ballinger could not control her irritation. 'Really, it is too bad that we should not be able to talk the matter over quietly among ourselves. Personally, I think that if one goes into Xingu at all—'

'Oh, so do I!' cried Miss Glyde.

'And I don't see how one can avoid doing so, if one wishes to keep up with the Thought of the Day—'

Mrs Leveret uttered an exclamation of relief. 'There – that's it!' she interposed.

'What's it?' the President took her up.

'Why – it's a – a Thought: I mean a philosophy.'

This seemed to bring a certain relief to Mrs Ballinger and Laura Glyde, but Miss Van Vluyck said: 'Excuse me if I tell you that you're all mistaken. Xingu happens to be a language.'

'A language!' the Lunch Club cried.

'Certainly. Don't you remember Fanny Roby's saying that there were several branches, and that some were hard to trace? What could that apply to but dialects?'

Mrs Ballinger could no longer restrain a contemptuous laugh. 'Really, if the Lunch Club has reached such a pass that it has to go to Fanny Roby for instruction on a subject like Xingu, it had almost better cease to exist!'

'It's really her fault for not being clearer,' Laura Glyde put in.

'Oh, clearness and Fanny Roby!' Mrs Ballinger shrugged. 'I daresay we shall find she was mistaken on almost every point.'

'Why not look it up?' said Mrs Plinth.

As a rule this recurrent suggestion of Mrs Plinth's was ignored in the heat of discussion, and only resorted to afterward in the privacy of each member's home. But on the present occasion the desire to ascribe their own confusion of thought to the vague and contradictory nature of Mrs Roby's statements caused the members of the Lunch Club to utter a collective demand for a book of reference.

At this point the production of her treasured volume gave Mrs Leveret, for a moment, the unusual experience of occupying the centre front; but she was not able to hold it long, for *Appropriate Allusions* contained no mention of Xingu.

'Oh, that's not the kind of thing we want!' exclaimed Miss Van Vluyck. She cast a disparaging glance over Mrs Ballinger's assortment of literature, and added impatiently: 'Haven't you any useful books?'

'Of course I have,' replied Mrs Ballinger indignantly; 'I keep them in my husband's dressing-room.'

From this region, after some difficulty and delay, the parlour-maid produced the W-Z volume of an Encyclopaedia and, in deference to the fact that the demand for it had come from Miss Van Vluyck, laid the ponderous tome before her.

There was a moment of painful suspense while Miss Van Vluyck rubbed her spectacles, adjusted them, and turned to Z; and a murmur of surprise when she said: 'It isn't here.'

'I suppose,' said Mrs Plinth, 'it's not fit to be put in a book of reference.'

'Oh, nonsense!' exclaimed Mrs Ballinger. 'Try X.'

Miss Van Vluyck turned back through the volume, peering short-sightedly up and down the pages, till she came to a stop and remained motionless, like a dog on a point.

'Well, have you found it?' Mrs Ballinger enquired after a considerable delay.

'Yes. I've found it,' said Miss Van Vluyck in a queer voice.

Mrs Plinth hastily interposed: 'I beg you won't read it aloud if there's anything offensive.'

Miss Van Vluyck, without answering, continued her silent scrutiny.

'Well, what *is* it?' exclaimed Laura Glyde excitedly.

'*Do* tell us!' urged Mrs Leveret, feeling that she would have something awful to tell her sister.

Miss Van Vluyck pushed the volume aside and turned slowly toward the expectant group.

'It's a river.'

'A *river*?'

'Yes: in Brazil. Isn't that where she's been living?'

'Who? Fanny Roby? Oh, but you must be mistaken. You've been reading the wrong thing,' Mrs Ballinger exclaimed, leaning over her to seize the volume.

'It's the only Xingu in the Encyclopaedia; and she *has* been living in Brazil,' Miss Van Vluyck persisted.

'Yes: her brother has a consulship there,' Mrs Leveret interposed.

'But it's too ridiculous! I – we – why we *all* remember studying Xingu last year – or the year before last,' Mrs Ballinger stammered.

'I thought I did when *you* said so,' Laura Glyde avowed.

'I said so?' cried Mrs Ballinger.

'Yes. You said it had crowded everything else out of your mind.'

'Well *you* said it had changed your whole life!'

'For that matter, Miss Van Vluyck said she had never grudged the time she'd given it.'

Mrs Plinth interposed: 'I made it clear that I knew nothing whatever of the original.'

Mrs Ballinger broke off the dispute with a groan. 'Oh, what does it all matter if she's been making fools of us? I believe Miss Van Vluyck's right – she was talking of the river all the while!'

'How could she? It's too preposterous,' Miss Glyde exclaimed.

'Listen.' Miss Van Vluyck had repossessed herself of the Encyclopaedia, and restored her spectacles to a nose reddened by excitement. ' "The Xingu, one of the principal rivers of Brazil, rises on the plateau of Mato Grosso, and flows in a northerly direction for a length of no less than one thousand one hundred and eighteen miles, entering the Amazon near the mouth of the latter river. The upper course of the Xingu is auriferous and fed by numerous branches. Its source was first discovered in 1884 by the German explorer von den Steinen, after a difficult and dangerous expedition through a region inhabited by tribes still in the Stone Age of culture." '

The ladies received this communication in a state of stupefied silence from which Mrs Leveret was the first to rally. 'She certainly *did* speak of its having branches.'

The word seemed to snap the last thread of their incredulity. 'And of its great length,' gasped Mrs Ballinger.

'She said it was awfully deep, and you couldn't skip – you just had to wade through,' Miss Glyde added.

The idea worked its way more slowly through Mrs Plinth's compact resistances. 'How could there be anything improper about a river?' she enquired.

'Improper?'

'Why, what she said about the source – that it was corrupt?'

'Not corrupt, but hard to get at,' Laura Glyde corrected. 'Someone who'd been there had told her so. I daresay it was the explorer himself – doesn't it say the expedition was dangerous?'

' "Difficult and dangerous",' read Miss Van Vluyck.

Mrs Ballinger pressed her hands to her throbbing temples. 'There's nothing she said that wouldn't apply to a river – to this river!' She swung about excitedly to the other members. 'Why, do you remember her telling us that she hadn't read *The Supreme Instant* because she'd taken it on a boating-party while she was staying with her brother, and someone had "shied" it overboard – "shied" of course was her own expression.'

The ladies breathlessly signified that the expression had not escaped them.

'Well – and then didn't she tell Osric Dane that one of her books was simply saturated with Xingu? Of course it was, if one of Mrs Roby's rowdy friends had thrown it into the river!'

This surprising reconstruction of the scene in which they had just participated left the members of the Lunch Club inarticulate. At length, Mrs Plinth, after visibly labouring with the problem, said in a heavy tone: 'Osric Dane was taken in too.'

Mrs Leveret took courage at this. 'Perhaps that's what Mrs Roby did it for. She said Osric Dane was a brute, and she may have wanted to give her a lesson.'

Miss Van Vluyck frowned. 'It was hardly worth while to do it at our expense.'

'At least,' said Miss Glyde with a touch of bitterness, 'she succeeded in interesting her, which was more than we did.'

'What chance had we?' rejoined Mrs Ballinger.

'Mrs Roby monopolised her from the first. And *that*, I've no doubt, was her purpose – to give Osric Dane a false impression of her own standing in the club. She would hesitate at nothing to attract attention: we all know how she took in poor Professor Foreland.'

'She actually makes him give bridge-teas every Thursday,' Mrs Leveret piped up.

Laura Glyde struck her hands together. 'Why, this is Thursday, and it's *there* she's gone, of course; and taken Osric with her!'

'And they're shrieking over us at this moment,' said Mrs Ballinger between her teeth.

This possibility seemed too preposterous to be admitted. 'She would hardly dare,' said Miss Van Vluyck, 'confess the imposture to Osric Dane.'

'I'm not so sure: I thought I saw her make a sign as she left. If she hadn't made a sign, why should Osric Dane have rushed out after her?'

'Well, you know, we'd all been telling her how wonderful Xingu was, and she said she wanted to find out more about it,' Mrs Leveret said, with a tardy impulse of justice to the absent.

This reminder, far from mitigating the wrath of the other members, gave it a stronger impetus.

'Yes – and that's exactly what they're both laughing over now,' said Laura Glyde ironically.

Mrs Plinth stood up and gathered her expensive furs about her monumental form. 'I have no wish to criticise,' she said; 'but unless the Lunch Club can protect its members against the recurrence of such – such unbecoming scenes, I for one—'

'Oh, so do I!' agreed Miss Glyde, rising also.

Miss Van Vluyck closed the Encyclopaedia and proceeded to button herself into her jacket. 'My time is really too valuable—' she began.

'I fancy we are all of one mind,' said Mrs Ballinger, looking searchingly at Mrs Leveret, who looked at the others.

'I always deprecate anything like a scandal—' Mrs Plinth continued.

'She has been the cause of one to-day!' exclaimed Miss Glyde.

Mrs Leveret moaned: 'I don't see how she *could!*' and Miss Van Vluyck said, picking up her note-book: 'Some women stop at nothing.'

'—but if,' Mrs Plinth took up her argument impressively, 'anything of the kind had happened in *my* house' (it never would have, her tone implied), 'I should have felt that I owed it to myself either to ask for Mrs Roby's resignation – or to offer mine.'

'Oh, Mrs Plinth—' gasped the Lunch Club.

'Fortunately for me,' Mrs Plinth continued with an awful magnanimity, 'the matter was taken out of my hands by our President's decision that the right to entertain distinguished guests was a privilege vested in her office; and I think the other members will agree that, as she was alone in this opinion, she ought to be alone in deciding on the best way of effacing its – its really deplorable consequences.'

A deep silence followed this outbreak of Mrs Plinth's long-stored resentment.

'I don't see why I should be expected to ask her to resign—' Mrs Ballinger at length began; but Laura Glyde turned back to remind her: 'You know she made you say that you'd got on swimmingly in Xingu.'

An ill-timed giggle escaped from Mrs Leveret, and Mrs Ballinger energetically continued '—but you needn't think for a moment that I'm afraid to!'

The door of the drawing-room closed on the retreating backs of the Lunch Club, and the President of that distinguished association, seating herself at her writing-table, and pushing away a copy of *The Wings of Death* to make room for her elbow, drew forth a sheet of the club's note-paper, on which she began to write: 'My dear Mrs Roby—'

Heidi *(excerpt)*

JOHANNA SPYRI

As soon as Dete had disappeared the old man went back to his bench, and there he remained seated, staring on the ground without uttering a sound, while thick curls of smoke floated upward from his pipe. Heidi, meanwhile, was enjoying herself in her new surroundings; she looked about till she found a shed, built against the hut, where the goats were kept; she peeped in, and saw it was empty. She continued her search and presently came to the fir trees behind the hut. A strong breeze was blowing through them, and there was a rushing and roaring in their topmost branches, Heidi stood still and listened. The sound growing fainter, she went on again, to the farther corner of the hut, and so round to where her grandfather was sitting. Seeing that he was in exactly the same position as when she left him, she went and placed herself in front of the old man, and putting her hands behind her back, stood and gazed at him. Her grandfather looked up, and as she continued standing there without moving, 'What is it you want?' he asked.

'I want to see what you have inside the house,' said Heidi.

'Come then!' and the grandfather rose and went before her towards the hut.

'Bring your bundle of clothes in with you,' he bid her as she was following.

'I shan't want them any more,' was her prompt answer.

The old man turned and looked searchingly at the child, whose dark eyes were sparkling in delighted anticipation of what she was going to see inside. 'She is certainly not wanting in intelligence,' he murmured to himself. 'And why shall you not want them any more?' he asked aloud.

'Because I want to go about like the goats with their thin light legs.'

'Well, you can do so if you like,' said her grandfather, 'but bring the things in, we must put them in the cupboard.'

Heidi did as she was told. The old man now opened the door and Heidi stepped inside after him; she found herself in a good-sized room, which covered the whole ground floor of the hut. A table and a chair were the only furniture; in one corner stood the grandfather's bed, in another was the hearth with a large kettle hanging above it; and on the further side was a large door in the wall – this was the cupboard. The grandfather opened it; inside were his clothes, some hanging up, others, a couple of shirts, and some socks and handkerchiefs, lying on a shelf; on a second shelf were some plates and cups and glasses, and on a higher one still, a round loaf, smoked meat, and cheese, for everything that Alm-Uncle needed for his food and clothing was kept in this cupboard. Heidi, as soon as it was opened, ran quickly forward and thrust in her bundle of clothes, as far back behind her grandfather's things as possible, so that they might not easily be found again. She then looked carefully round the room, and asked, 'Where am I to sleep, grandfather?'

'Wherever you like,' he answered.

Heidi was delighted, and began at once to examine all the nooks and corners to find out where it would be pleasantest to sleep. In the corner near her grandfather's bed she saw a short ladder against the wall; up she climbed and found herself in the hayloft. There lay a large heap of fresh sweet-smelling hay, while through a round window in the wall she could see right down the valley.

'I shall sleep up here, grandfather,' she called down to him. 'It's lovely, up here. Come up and see how lovely it is!'

'Oh, I know all about it,' he called up in answer.

'I am getting the bed ready now,' she called down again, as she went busily to and fro at her work, 'but I shall want you to bring me up a sheet; you can't have a bed without a sheet, you want it to lie upon.'

'All right,' said the grandfather, and presently he went to the cupboard, and after rummaging about inside for a few minutes he drew out a long, coarse piece of stuff, which was all he had to do duty for a sheet. He carried it up to the loft, where he found Heidi had already made quite a nice bed. She had put an extra heap of hay at one end for a pillow, and had so arranged it that, when in bed, she would be able to see comfortably out through the round window.

'That is capital,' said her grandfather; 'now we must put on the sheet, but wait a moment first,' and he went and fetched another large bundle of hay to make the bed thicker, so that the child should not feel the hard floor under her – 'there, now bring it here.' Heidi had got hold of the sheet, but it was almost too heavy for her to carry; this was a good thing, however, as the close thick stuff would prevent the sharp stalks of the hay running through and pricking her. The two together now spread the sheet over the bed, and where it was too long or too broad, Heidi quickly tucked it in under the hay. It looked now as tidy and comfortable a bed as you could wish for, and Heidi stood gazing thoughtfully at her handiwork.

'We have forgotten something now, grandfather,' she said after a short silence.

'What's that?' he asked.

'A coverlid; when you get into bed, you have to creep in between the sheets and the coverlid.'

'Oh, that's the way, is it? But suppose I have not got a coverlid?' said the old man.

'Well, never mind, grandfather,' said Heidi in a consoling tone of voice, 'I can take some more hay to put over me,' and she was turning quickly to fetch another armful from the heap, when her grandfather stopped her. 'Wait a moment,' he said, and he climbed down the ladder again and went towards his bed. He returned to the loft with a large, thick sack, made of flax, which he threw down, exclaiming, 'There, that is better than hay, is it not?'

Heidi began tugging away at the sack with all her little might, in her efforts to get it smooth and straight, but her small hands were not fitted for so heavy a job. Her grandfather came to her assistance, and when they had got it tidily spread over the bed, it all looked so nice and warm and comfortable that Heidi stood gazing at it in delight. 'That is a splendid coverlid,' she said, 'and the bed looks lovely altogether! I wish it was night, so that I might get inside it at once.'

'I think we might have something to eat first,' said the grandfather, 'what do you think?'

Heidi in the excitement of bed-making had forgotten everything else; but now when she began to think about food she felt terribly hungry, for she had had nothing to eat since the piece of bread and little cup of thin coffee that had been her breakfast early that morning before starting on her long, hot journey. So she answered without hesitation, 'Yes, I think so too.'

'Let us go down then, as we both think alike,' said the old man, and he followed the child down the ladder. Then he went up to the hearth, pushed the big kettle aside, and drew forward the little one that was hanging on the chain, and seating himself on the round-topped, three-legged stool before the fire, blew it up into a clear bright flame. The kettle soon began to boil, and meanwhile the old man held a large piece of cheese on a long iron fork over the fire, turning it round and round till it was toasted a nice golden yellow colour on each side. Heidi watched all that was going on with eager curiosity. Suddenly some new idea seemed to come into her head, for she turned and ran to the cupboard, and then began going busily backwards and forwards. Presently the grandfather got up and came to the table with a jug and the cheese, and there he saw it already tidily laid with the round loaf and two plates and two knives each in its right place;

for Heidi had taken exact note that morning of all that there was in the cupboard, and she knew which things would be wanted for their meal.

'Ah, that's right,' said the grandfather, 'I am glad to see that you have some ideas of your own,' and as he spoke he laid the toasted cheese on a layer of bread, 'but there is still something missing.'

Heidi looked at the jug that was steaming away invitingly, and ran quickly back to the cupboard. At first she could only see a small bowl left on the shelf, but she was not long in perplexity, for a moment later she caught sight of two glasses further back, and without an instant's loss of time she returned with these and the bowl and put them down on the table.

'Good, I see you know how to set about things; but what will you do for a seat?' The grandfather himself was sitting on the only chair in the room. Heidi flew to the hearth, and dragging the three-legged stool up to the table, sat herself down upon it.

'Well, you have managed to find a seat for yourself, I see, only rather a low one I am afraid,' said the grandfather, 'but you would not be tall enough to reach the table even if you sat in my chair; the first thing now, however, is to have something to eat, so come along.'

With that he stood up, filled the bowl with milk, and placing it on the chair, pushed it in front of Heidi on her little three-legged stool, so that she now had a table to herself. Then he brought her a large slice of bread and a piece of the golden cheese, and told her to eat. After which he went and sat down on the corner of the table and began his own meal. Heidi lifted the bowl with both hands and drank without pause till it was empty, for the thirst of all her long hot journey had returned upon her. Then she drew a deep breath – in the eagerness of her thirst she had not stopped to breathe – and put down the bowl.

'Was the milk nice?' asked her grandfather.

'I never drank any so good before,' answered Heidi.

'Then you must have some more,' and the old man filled her bowl again to the brim and set it before the child, who was now hungrily beginning her bread having first spread it with the cheese, which after being toasted was soft as butter; the two together tasted deliciously, and the child looked the picture of content as she sat eating, and at intervals taking further draughts of milk. The meal being over, the grandfather went outside to put the goat-shed in order, and Heidi watched with interest while he first swept it out, and then put fresh straw for the goats to sleep upon. Then he went to the little well-shed, and there he cut some long round sticks, and a small round board; in this he bored some holes and stuck the sticks into them, and there, as if made by magic, was a three-legged stool just like her grand-father's, only higher. Heidi stood and looked at it, speechless with astonishment.

'What do you think that is?' asked her grandfather.

'It's my stool, I know, because it is such a high one; and it was made all of a minute,' said the child, still lost in wonder and admiration.

'She understands what she sees, her eyes are in the right place,' remarked the grandfather to himself, as he continued his way round the hut, knocking in a nail here and there, or making fast some part of the door, and so with hammer and nails and pieces of wood going from spot to spot, mending or clearing away wherever work of the kind was needed. Heidi followed him step by step, her eyes attentively taking in all that he did, and everything that she saw was a fresh source of pleasure to her.

And so the time passed happily on till evening. Then the wind began to roar louder than ever through the old fir trees; Heidi listened with delight to the sound, and it filled her heart so full of gladness that she skipped and danced round the old trees, as if some unheard of joy had come to her. The grandfather stood and watched her from the shed.

Suddenly a shrill whistle was heard. Heidi paused in her dancing, and the grandfather came out. Down from the heights above the goats came springing one after another, with Peter in their midst. Heidi sprang forward with a cry of joy and rushed among the flock, greeting first one and then another of her old friends of the morning. As they neared the hut the goats stood still, and then two of their number, two beautiful slender animals, one white and one brown, ran forward to where the grandfather was standing and began licking his hands, for he was holding a little salt which he always had ready for his goats on their return home. Peter disappeared with the remainder of his flock. Heidi tenderly stroked the two goats in turn, running first to one side of them and then the other, and jumping about in her glee at the pretty little animals. 'Are they ours, grandfather? Are they both ours? Are you going to put them in the shed? Will they always stay with us?'

Heidi's questions came tumbling out one after the other, so that her grandfather had only time to answer each of them with

'Yes, yes.' When the goats had finished licking up the salt her grandfather told her to go and fetch her bowl and the bread.

Heidi obeyed and was soon back again. The grandfather milked the white goat and filled her basin, and then breaking off a piece of bread, 'Now eat your supper,' he said, 'and then go up to bed. Cousin Dete left another little bundle for you with a nightgown and other small things in it, which you will find at the bottom of the cupboard if you want them. I must go and shut up the goats, so be off and sleep well.'

'Good-night, grandfather! good-night. What are their names, grandfather, what are their names?' she called out as she ran after his retreating figure and the goats.

'The white one is named Little Swan, and the brown one Little Bear,' he answered.

'Good-night, Little Swan, good-night, Little Bear!' she called again at the top of her voice, for they were already inside the shed. Then she sat down on the seat and began to eat and drink, but the wind was so strong that it almost blew her away; so she made haste and finished her supper and then went indoors and climbed up to her bed, where she was soon lying as sweetly and soundly asleep as any young princess on her couch of silk.

Not long after, and while it was still twilight, the grandfather also went to bed, for he was up every morning at sunrise, and the sun came climbing up over the mountains at a very early hour during these summer months. The wind grew so tempestuous during the night, and blew in such gusts against the walls, that the hut trembled and the old beams groaned and creaked. It came howling and wailing down the chimney like voices of those in pain, and it raged with such fury among the old fir trees that here and there a branch was snapped and fell. In the middle of the night the old man got up. 'The child will be frightened,' he murmured half aloud. He mounted the ladder and went and stood by the child's bed.

Outside the moon was struggling with the dark, fast-driving clouds, which at one moment left it clear and shining, and the next swept over it, and all again was dark. Just now the moonlight was falling through the round window straight on to Heidi's bed. She lay under the heavy coverlid, her cheeks rosy with sleep, her head peacefully resting on her little round arm, and with a happy expression on her baby face as if dreaming of something pleasant. The old man stood looking down on the sleeping child until the moon again disappeared behind the clouds and he could see no more, then he went back to bed.

From 'Bacchanalia'

MATTHEW ARNOLD

The evening comes, the fields are still.
The tinkle of the thirsty rill,
Unheard all day, ascends again;
Deserted is the half-mown plain,
Silent the swaths! the ringing wain,
The mower's cry, the dog's alarms,
All housed within the sleeping farms!
The business of the day is done,
The last-left haymaker is gone.
And from the thyme upon the height,
And from the elder-blossom white
And pale dog-roses in the hedge,
And from the mint-plant in the sedge,
In puffs of balm the night-air blows
The perfume which the day forgoes.

And on the pure horizon far,
See, pulsing with the first-born star,
The liquid sky above the hill!
The evening comes, the fields are still.

Loitering and leaping,
With saunter, with bounds –
Flickering and circling
In files and in rounds –
Gaily their pine-staff green
Tossing in air,
Loose o'er their shoulders white
Showering their hair –
See! the wild Maenads
Break from the wood,
Youth and Iacchus
Maddening their blood.

See! through the quiet land
Rioting they pass –
Fling the fresh heaps about,
Trample the grass.

Tear from the rifled hedge
Garlands, their prize;
Fill with their sports the field,
Fill with their cries.

Shepherd, what ails thee, then?
Shepherd, why mute?
Forth with thy joyous song!
Forth with thy flute!
Tempts not the revel blithe?
Lure not their cries?
Glow not their shoulders smooth?
Melt not their eyes?
Is not, on cheeks like those,
Lovely the flush?
– *Ah, so the quiet was!*
So was the hush!

Three Questions

LEO TOLSTOY, *trans.* AYLMER & LOUISE MAUDE

*I*t once occurred to a certain king, that if he always knew the right time to begin everything; if he knew who were the right people to listen to, and whom to avoid; and, above all, if he always knew what was the most important thing to do, he would never fail in anything he might undertake.

And this thought having occurred to him, he had it proclaimed throughout his kingdom that he would give a great reward to anyone who would teach him what was the right time for every action, and who were the most necessary people, and how he might know what was the most important thing to do.

And learned men came to the King, but they all answered his questions differently.

In reply to the first question, some said that to know the right time for every action, one must draw up in advance, a table of days, months and years, and must live strictly according to it. Only thus, said they, could everything be done at its proper time. Others declared that it was impossible to decide beforehand the right time for every action; but that, not letting oneself be absorbed in idle pastimes, one should always attend to all that was going on, and then do what was most needful. Others, again, said that however attentive the King might be to what was going on, it was impossible for one man to decide correctly the right time for every action, but that he should have a Council of wise men, who would help him to fix the proper time for everything.

But then again others said there were some things which could not wait to be laid before a Council, but about which one had at once to decide whether to undertake them or not. But in order to decide that, one must know beforehand what was going to happen. It is only magicians who know that; and, therefore, in order to know the right time for every action, one must consult magicians.

Equally various were the answers to the second question. Some said, the people the King most needed were his councillors; others, the priests; others, the doctors; while some said the warriors were the most necessary.

To the third question, as to what was the most important occupation: some replied that the most important thing in the world was science. Others said it was skill in warfare; and others, again, that it was religious worship.

All the answers being different, the King agreed with none of them, and gave the reward to none. But still wishing to find the right answers to his questions, he decided to consult a hermit, widely renowned for his wisdom.

The hermit lived in a wood which he never quitted, and he received none but common folk. So the King put on simple clothes, and before reaching the hermit's cell dismounted from his horse, and, leaving his body-guard behind, went on alone.

When the King approached, the hermit was digging the ground in front of his hut. Seeing the King, he greeted him and went on digging. The hermit was frail and weak, and each time he stuck his spade into the ground and turned a little earth, he breathed heavily.

The King went up to him and said: 'I have come to you, wise hermit, to ask you to answer three questions: How can I learn to do the right thing at the right time? Who are the people I most need, and to whom should I, therefore, pay more attention than to the rest? And, what affairs are the most important, and need my first attention?'

The hermit listened to the King, but answered nothing. He just spat on his hand and recommenced digging.

'You are tired,' said the King, 'let me take the spade and work awhile for you.'

'Thanks!' said the hermit, and, giving the spade to the King, he sat down on the ground.

When he had dug two beds, the King stopped and repeated his questions. The hermit again gave no answer, but rose, stretched out his hand for the spade, and said:

'Now rest awhile – and let me work a bit.'

But the King did not give him the spade, and continued to dig. One hour passed, and another. The sun began to sink behind the trees, and the King at last stuck the spade into the ground, and said:

'I came to you, wise man, for an answer to my questions. If you can give me none, tell me so, and I will return home.'

'Here comes someone running,' said the hermit, 'let us see who it is.'

The King turned round, and saw a bearded man come running out of the wood. The man held his hands pressed against his stomach, and blood was flowing from under them. When he reached the King, he fell fainting on the ground moaning feebly. The King and the hermit unfastened the man's clothing. There was a large wound in his stomach. The King washed it as best he could, and bandaged it with his handkerchief and with a towel the hermit had. But the blood would not stop flowing, and the King again and again removed the bandage soaked with warm blood, and washed and rebandaged the wound. When at last the blood ceased flowing, the man revived and asked for something to drink. The King brought fresh water and gave it to him. Meanwhile the sun had set, and it had become cool. So the King, with the hermit's help, carried the wounded man into the hut and laid him on the bed. Lying on the bed the man closed his eyes and was quiet; but the King was so tired with his walk and with the work he had done, that he crouched down on the threshold, and also fell asleep – so soundly that he slept all through the short summer night. When he awoke in the morning, it was long before he could remember where he was, or who was the strange bearded man lying on the bed and gazing intently at him with shining eyes.

'Forgive me!' said the bearded man in a weak voice, when he saw that the King was awake and was looking at him.

'I do not know you, and have nothing to forgive you for,' said the King.

'You do not know me, but I know you. I am that enemy of yours who swore to revenge himself on you, because you executed his brother and seized his property. I knew you had gone alone to see the hermit, and I resolved to kill you on your way back. But the day passed and you did not return. So I came out from my ambush to find you, and I came upon your bodyguard, and they recognised me, and wounded me. I escaped from them, but should have bled to death had you not dressed my wound. I wished to kill you, and you have saved my life. Now, if I live, and if you wish it, I will serve you as your most faithful slave, and will bid my sons do the same. Forgive me!'

The King was very glad to have made peace with his enemy so easily, and to have gained him for a friend, and he not only forgave him, but said he would send his servants and his own physician to attend him, and promised to restore his property.

Having taken leave of the wounded man, the King went out into the porch and looked around for the hermit. Before going away he wished once more to beg an answer to the questions he had put. The hermit was outside, on his knees, sowing seeds in the beds that had been dug the day before.

The King approached him, and said:

'For the last time, I pray you to answer my questions, wise man.'

'You have already been answered!' said the hermit, still crouching on his thin legs, and looking up at the King, who stood before him.

'How answered? What do you mean?' asked the King.

'Do you not see,' replied the hermit. 'If you had not pitied my weakness yesterday, and had not dug those beds for me, but had gone your way, that man would have attacked you, and you would have repented of not having stayed with me. So the most important time was when you were digging the beds; and I was the most important man; and to do me good was your most important business. Afterwards when that man ran to us, the most important time was when you were attending to him, for if you had not bound up his wounds he would have died without having made peace with you. So he was the most important man, and what you did for him was your most important business. Remember then: there is only one time that is important – Now! It is the most important time because it is the only time when we have any power. The most necessary man is he with whom you are, for no man knows whether he will ever have dealings with anyone else: and the most important affair is, to do him good, because for that purpose alone was man sent into this life!'

Far Away and Long Ago *(excerpt)*

W. H. HUDSON

What, then, did I want? – what did I ask to have? If the question had been put to me then, and if I had been capable of expressing what was in me, I should have replied: I want only to keep what I have; to rise each morning and look out on the sky and the grassy dew-wet earth from day to day, from year to year. To watch every June and July for spring, to feel the same old sweet surprise and delight at the appearance of each familiar flower, every new-born insect, every bird returned once more from the north. To listen in a trance of delight to the wild notes of the golden plover coming once more to the great plain, flying, flying south, flock succeeding flock the whole day long. Oh, those wild beautiful cries of the golden plover! I could exclaim with Hafiz, with but one word changed: 'If after a thousand years that sound should float o'er my tomb, my bones uprising in their gladness would dance in the sepulchre!' To climb trees and put my hand down in the deep hot nest of the Bien-te-veo and feel the hot eggs – the five long pointed cream-coloured eggs with chocolate spots and splashes at the larger end. To lie on a grassy bank with the blue water between me and beds of tall bulrushes, listening to the mysterious sounds of the wind and of hidden rails and coots and courlans conversing together in strange human-like tones; to let my sight dwell and feast on the *camaloté* flower amid its floating masses of moist vivid green leaves – the large alamanda-like flower of a purest divine yellow that when plucked sheds its lovely petals, to leave you with nothing but a green stem in your hand. To ride at noon on the hottest days, when the whole earth is a-glitter with illusory water, and see the cattle and horses in thousands, covering the plain at their watering-places; to visit some haunt of large birds at that still, hot hour and see storks, ibises, grey herons, egrets of a dazzling whiteness, and rose-coloured spoonbills and flamingoes, standing in the shallow water in which their motionless forms are reflected. To lie on my back on the rust-brown grass in January and gaze up at the wide hot whitey-blue sky, peopled with millions and myriads of glistening balls of thistledown, ever, ever floating by; to gaze and gaze until they are to me living things and I, in an ecstasy, am with them, floating in that immense shining void!

Anne of Green Gables *(excerpt)*

L. M. MONTGOMERY

Anne was bringing the cows home from the back pasture by way of Lover's Lane. It was a September evening and all the gaps and clearings in the woods were brimmed up with ruby sunset light. Here and there the lane was splashed with it, but for the most part it was already quite shadowy beneath the maples, and the spaces under the firs were filled with a clear violet dusk like airy wine. The winds were out in their tops, and there is no sweeter music on earth than that which the wind makes in the fir trees at evening.

The cows swung placidly down the lane, and Anne followed them dreamily, repeating aloud the battle canto from *Marmion* – which had also been part of their English course the preceding winter and which Miss Stacy had made them learn off by heart – and exulting in its rushing lines and the clash of spears in its imagery. When she came to the lines

The stubborn spearsmen still made good
Their dark impenetrable wood,

she stopped in ecstasy to shut her eyes that she might the better fancy herself one of that heroic ring. When she opened them again it was to behold Diana coming through the gate that led into the Barry field and looking so important that Anne instantly divined there was news to be told. But betray too eager curiosity she would not.

'Isn't this evening just like a purple dream, Diana? It makes me so glad to be alive. In the mornings I always think the mornings are best; but when evening comes I think it's lovelier still.'

'It's a very fine evening,' said Diana, 'but oh, I have such news, Anne. Guess. You can have three guesses.'

'Charlotte Gillis is going to be married in the church after all and Mrs Allan wants us to decorate it,' cried Anne.

'No. Charlotte's beau won't agree to that, because nobody ever has been married in the church yet, and he thinks it would seem too much like a funeral. It's too mean, because it would be such fun. Guess again.'

'Jane's mother is going to let her have a birthday party?'

Diana shook her head, her black eyes dancing with merriment.

'I can't think what it can be,' said Anne in despair, 'unless it's that Moody Spurgeon MacPherson saw you home from prayer meeting last night. Did he?'

'I should think not,' exclaimed Diana indignantly. 'I wouldn't be likely to boast of it if he did, the horrid creature! I knew you couldn't guess it. Mother had a letter from Aunt Josephine today, and Aunt Josephine wants you and me to go to town next Tuesday and stop with her for the Exhibition. There!'

'Oh, Diana,' whispered Anne, finding it necessary to lean up against a maple tree for support, 'do you really mean it? But I'm afraid Marilla won't let me go. She will say that she can't encourage gadding about. That was what she said last week when Jane invited me to go with them in their double-seated buggy to the American concert at the White Sands Hotel. I wanted to go, but Marilla said I'd be better at home learning my lessons and so would Jane. I was bitterly disappointed, Diana. I felt so heartbroken that I wouldn't say my prayers when I went to bed. But I repented of that and got up in the middle of the night and said them.'

'I'll tell you,' said Diana, 'we'll get Mother to ask Marilla. She'll be more likely to let you go then; and if she does we'll have the time of our lives, Anne. I've never been to an Exhibition, and it's so aggravating to hear the other girls talking about their trips. Jane and Ruby have been twice, and they're going this year again.'

'I'm not going to think about it at all until I know whether I can go or not,' said Anne resolutely. 'If I did and then was disappointed, it would be more than I could bear. But in case I do go I'm very glad my new coat will be ready by that time. Marilla didn't think I needed a new coat. She said my old one would do very well for another winter and that I ought to be satisfied with having a new dress. The dress is very pretty, Diana – navy blue and made so fashionably. Marilla always makes my dresses fashionably now, because she says she doesn't intend to have Matthew going to Mrs Lynde to make them. I'm so glad. It is ever so much easier to be good if your clothes are fashionable. At least, it is easier for me. I suppose it doesn't make such a difference to naturally good people. But Matthew said I must have a new coat, so Marilla bought a lovely piece of blue broadcloth, and it's being made by a real dressmaker over at Carmody. It's to be done Saturday night, and I'm trying not to imagine myself walking up the church aisle on Sunday in my new suit and cap, because I'm afraid it isn't right to imagine such things. But it just slips into my mind in spite of me. My cap is so pretty. Matthew bought it for me the day we were over at Carmody. It is one of those little blue velvet ones that are all the rage, with gold cord and tassels. Your new hat is elegant, Diana, and so becoming. When I saw you come into church last Sunday my heart swelled with pride to think you were my dearest friend. Do you suppose it's wrong for us to think so much about our clothes? Marilla says it is very sinful. But it is such an interesting subject, isn't it?'

Marilla agreed to let Anne go to town, and it was arranged that Mr Barry should take the girls in on the following Tuesday. As Charlottetown was thirty miles away and Mr Barry wished to go and return the same day, it was necessary to make a very early start. But Anne counted it all joy, and was up before sunrise on Tuesday morning. A glance from her window assured her that the day would be fine, for the eastern sky behind the firs of the Haunted Wood was all silvery and cloudless. Through the gap in the trees a light was shining in the western gable of Orchard Slope, a token that Diana was also up.

Anne was dressed by the time Matthew had the fire on and had the breakfast ready when Marilla came down, but for her own part was much too excited to eat. After breakfast the jaunty new cap and jacket were donned, and Anne hastened over the brook and up through the firs to Orchard Slope. Mr Barry and Diana were waiting for her, and they were soon on the road.

It was a long drive, but Anne and Diana enjoyed every minute of it. It was delightful to rattle along over the moist roads in the early red sunlight that was creeping across the shorn harvest fields. The air was fresh and crisp, and little smoke-blue mists curled through the valleys and floated off from the hills. Sometimes the road went through woods where maples were beginning to hang out scarlet banners; sometimes it crossed rivers on bridges that made Anne's flesh cringe with the old, half-delightful fear; sometimes it wound along a harbour shore and passed by a little cluster of weather-grey fishing huts; again it mounted to hills whence a far sweep of curving upland or misty-blue sky could be seen; but wherever it went there was much of interest to discuss. It was almost noon when they reached town and found their way to 'Beechwood'. It was quite a fine old mansion, set back from the street in a seclusion of green elms and branching beeches. Miss Barry met them at the door with a twinkle in her sharp black eyes.

'So you've come to see me at last, you Anne-girl,' she said. 'Mercy, child, how you have grown! You're taller than I am, I declare. And you're ever so much better looking than you used to be, too. But I dare say you know that without being told.'

'Indeed I didn't,' said Anne radiantly. 'I know I'm not so freckled as I used to be, so I've much to be thankful for, but I really hadn't dared to hope there was any other improvement. I'm so glad you think there is, Miss Barry.' Miss Barry's house was furnished with 'great magnificence', as Anne told Marilla afterward. The two little country girls were rather abashed by the splendour of the parlour where Miss Barry left them when she went to see about dinner.

'Isn't it just like a palace?' whispered Diana. 'I never was in Aunt Josephine's house before, and I'd no idea it was so grand. I just wish Julia Bell could see this – she puts on such airs about her mother's parlour.'

'Velvet carpet,' sighed Anne luxuriously, 'and silk curtains! I've dreamed of such things, Diana. But do you know I don't believe I feel very comfortable with them after all. There are so many things in this room and all so splendid that there is no scope for imagination. That is one consolation when you are poor – there are so many more things you can imagine about.'

Their sojourn in town was something that Anne and Diana dated from for years. From first to last it was crowded with delights.

On Wednesday Miss Barry took them to the Exhibition grounds and kept them there all day.

'It was splendid,' Anne related to Marilla later on. 'I never imagined anything so interesting. I don't really know which department was the most interesting. I think I liked the horses and the flowers and the fancywork best. Josie Pye took first prize for knitted lace. I was real glad she did. And I was glad that I felt glad, for it shows I'm improving, don't you think, Marilla, when I can rejoice in Josie's success? Mr Harmon Andrews took second prize for Gravenstein apples and Mr Bell took first prize for a pig. Diana said she thought it was ridiculous for a Sunday-school superintendent to take a prize in pigs, but I don't see why. Do you? She said she would always think of it after this when he was praying so solemnly. Clara Louise MacPherson took a prize for painting, and Mrs Lynde got first prize for homemade butter and cheese. So Avonlea was pretty well represented, wasn't it? Mrs Lynde was there that day, and I never knew how much I really liked her until I saw her familiar face among all those strangers. There were thousands of people there, Marilla. It made me feel dreadfully insignificant. And Miss Barry took us up to the grandstand to see the horse races. Mrs Lynde wouldn't go; she said horse racing was an abomination and, she being a church member, thought it her bounden duty to set a good example by staying away. But there were so many there I don't believe Mrs Lynde's absence would ever be noticed. I don't think, though, that I ought to go very often to horse races, because they *are* awfully fascinating. Diana got so excited that she offered to bet me ten cents that the red horse would win. I didn't believe he would, but I refused to bet, because I wanted to tell Mrs Allan all about everything, and I felt sure it wouldn't do to tell her that. It's always wrong to do anything you can't tell the minister's wife. It's as good as an extra conscience to have a minister's wife for your friend. And I was very glad I didn't bet, because the red horse *did* win, and I would have lost ten cents. So you see that virtue was its own reward. We saw a man go up in a balloon. I'd love to go up in a balloon, Marilla; it would be simply thrilling; and we saw a man selling fortunes. You paid him ten cents and a little bird picked out your fortune for you. Miss Barry gave Diana and me ten cents each to have our fortunes told. Mine was that I would marry a dark-complected man who was very wealthy, and I would go across water to live. I looked carefully at all the dark men I saw after that, but I didn't care much for any of them, and anyhow I suppose it's too early to be looking out for him yet. Oh, it was a never-to-be-forgotten day, Marilla. I was so tired I couldn't sleep at night. Miss Barry put us in the spare room, according to promise. It was an elegant room, Marilla, but somehow sleeping in a spare room isn't what I used to think it was. That's the worst of growing up, and I'm beginning to realise it. The things you wanted so much when you were a child don't seem half so wonderful to you when you get them.'

Thursday the girls had a drive in the park, and in the evening Miss Barry took them to a concert in the Academy of Music, where a noted prima donna was to sing. To Anne the evening was a glittering vision of delight.

'Oh, Marilla, it was beyond description. I was so excited I couldn't even talk, so you may know what it was like. I just sat in enraptured silence. Madame Selitsky was perfectly beautiful, and wore white satin and diamonds. But when she began to sing I never thought about anything else. Oh, I can't tell you how I felt. But it seemed to me that it could never be hard to be good any more. I felt like I do when I look up to the stars. Tears came into my eyes, but, oh, they were such happy tears. I was so sorry when it was all over, and I told Miss Barry I didn't see how I was ever to return to common life again. She said she thought if we went over to the restaurant across the street and had an ice cream it might help me. That sounded so prosaic; but to my surprise I found it true. The ice cream was delicious, Marilla, and it was so lovely and dissipated to be sitting there eating it at eleven o'clock at night. Diana said she believed she was born for city life. Miss Barry asked me what my opinion was, but I said I would have to think it over very seriously before I could tell her what I really thought. So I thought it over after I went to bed. That is the best time to think things out. And I came to the conclusion, Marilla, that I wasn't born for city life and that I was glad of it. It's nice to be eating ice cream at brilliant restaurants at eleven o'clock at night once in a while; but as a regular thing I'd rather be in the east gable at eleven, sound asleep, but kind of knowing even in my sleep that the stars were shining outside and that the wind was blowing in the firs across the brook. I told Miss Barry so at breakfast the next morning and she laughed. Miss Barry generally laughed at anything I said, even when I said the most solemn things. I don't think I liked it, Marilla, because I wasn't trying to be funny. But she is a most hospitable lady and treated us royally.'

Friday brought going-home time, and Mr Barry drove in for the girls.

'Well, I hope you've enjoyed yourselves,' said Miss Barry, as she bade them good-bye.

'Indeed we have,' said Diana.

'And you, Anne-girl?'

'I've enjoyed every minute of the time,' said Anne, throwing her arms impulsively about the old woman's neck and kissing her wrinkled cheek. Diana would never have dared to do such a thing and felt rather aghast at Anne's freedom. But Miss Barry was pleased, and she stood on her veranda and watched the buggy out of sight. Then she went back into her big house with a sigh. It seemed very lonely, lacking those fresh young lives. Miss Barry was a rather selfish old lady, if the truth must be told, and had never cared much for anybody but herself. She valued people only as they were of service to her or amused her. Anne had amused her, and consequently stood high in the old lady's good graces. But Miss Barry found herself thinking less about Anne's quaint speeches than of her fresh enthusiasms, her transparent emotions, her little winning ways, and the sweetness of her eyes and lips.

'I thought Marilla Cuthbert was an old fool when I heard she'd adopted a girl out of an orphan asylum,' she said to herself, 'but I guess she didn't make much of a mistake after all. If I'd a child like Anne in the house all the time I'd be a better and happier woman.'

Anne and Diana found the drive home as pleasant as the drive in – pleasanter, indeed, since there was the delightful consciousness of home waiting at the end of it. It was sunset when they passed through White Sands and turned into the shore road. Beyond, the Avonlea hills came out darkly against the saffron sky. Behind them the moon was rising out of the sea that grew all radiant and transfigured in her light. Every little cove along the curving road was a marvel of dancing ripples. The waves broke with a soft swish on the rocks below them, and the tang of the sea was in the strong, fresh air.

'Oh, but it's good to be alive and to be going home,' breathed Anne.

When she crossed the log bridge over the brook the kitchen light of Green Gables winked her a friendly welcome back, and through the open door shone the hearth fire, sending out its warm red glow athwart the chilly autumn night. Anne ran blithely up the hill and into the kitchen, where a hot supper was waiting on the table.

'So you've got back?' said Marilla, folding up her knitting.

'Yes, and oh, it's so good to be back,' said Anne joyously. 'I could kiss everything, even to the clock. Marilla, a broiled chicken! You don't mean to say you cooked that for me!'

'Yes, I did,' said Marilla. 'I thought you'd be hungry after such a drive and need something real appetising. Hurry and take off your things, and we'll have supper as soon as Matthew comes in. I'm glad you've got back, I must say. It's been fearful lonesome here without you, and I never put in four longer days.'

After supper Anne sat before the fire between Matthew and Marilla, and gave them a full account of her visit.

'I've had a splendid time,' she concluded happily, 'and I feel that it marks an epoch in my life. But the best of it all was the coming home.'

Night

WILLIAM BLAKE

The sun descending in the west;
　　The evening star does shine;
The birds are silent in their nest,
　　And I must seek for mine.
　　　　The moon, like a flower
　　　　In heaven's high bower,
　　　　With silent delight
　　　　Sits and smiles on the night.

Farewell, green fields and happy groves,
　　Where flocks have took delight,
Where lambs have nibbled, silent moves
　　The feet of angels bright;
　　　　Unseen, they pour blessing,
　　　　And joy without ceasing,
　　　　On each bud and blossom,
　　　　And each sleeping bosom.

They look in every thoughtless nest
   Where birds are covered warm;
They visit caves of every beast,
   To keep them all from harm:
      If they see any weeping
      That should have been sleeping,
      They pour sleep on their head,
      And sit down by their bed.

When wolves and tigers howl for prey,
   They pitying stand and weep;
Seeking to drive their thirst away,
   And keep them from the sheep.
      But, if they rush dreadful,
      The angels, most heedful,
      Receive each mild spirit,
      New worlds to inherit.

And there the lion's ruddy eyes
   Shall flow with tears of gold:
And pitying the tender cries,
   And walking round the fold:
      Saying: 'Wrath by His meekness,
      And, by His health, sickness,
      Is driven away
      From our immortal day.

'And now beside thee, bleating lamb,
   I can lie down and sleep,
Or think on Him who bore thy name,
   Graze after thee, and weep.
      For, washed in life's river,
      My bright mane for ever
      Shall shine like the gold,
      As I guard o'er the fold.'

'Meadow Thoughts', from
The Life of the Fields

RICHARD JEFFERIES

*T*he old house stood by the silent country road, secluded by many a long, long mile, and yet again secluded within the great walls of the garden. Often and often I rambled up to the milestone which stood under an oak, to look at the chipped inscription low down – 'To London, 79 Miles.' So far away, you see, that the very inscription was cut at the foot of the stone, since no one would be likely to want that information. It was half hidden by docks and nettles, despised and unnoticed. A broad land this seventy-nine miles – how many meadows and corn-fields, hedges and woods, in that distance? – wide enough to seclude any house, to hide it, like an acorn in the grass. Those who have lived all their lives in remote places do not feel the remoteness. No one else seemed to be conscious of the breadth that separated the place from the great centre, but it was, perhaps, that consciousness which deepened the solitude to me. It made the silence more still; the shadows of the oaks yet slower in their movement; everything more earnest. To convey a full impression of the intense concentration of Nature in the meadows is very difficult – everything is so utterly oblivious of man's thought and man's heart. The oaks stand – quiet, still – so still that the lichen loves them. At their feet the grass grows, and heeds nothing. Among it the squirrels leap, and their little hearts are as far away from you or me as the very wood of the oaks. The sunshine settles itself in the valley by the brook, and abides there whether we come or not. Glance through the gap in the hedge by the oak, and see how concentrated it is – all of it, every blade of grass, and leaf, and flower, and living creature, finch or squirrel. It is mesmerised upon itself. Then I used to feel that it really was seventy-nine miles to London, and not an hour or two only by rail, really all those miles. A great, broad province of green furrow and ploughed furrow between the old house and the city of the world. Such solace and solitude seventy-nine miles thick cannot be painted; the trees cannot be placed far enough away in perspective. It is necessary to stay in it like the oaks to know it.

Lime-tree branches overhung the corner of the garden-wall, whence a view was easy of the silent and dusty road, till over-arching oaks concealed it. The white dust heated by the sunshine, the green hedges, and the heavily massed trees, white clouds rolled together in the sky, a footpath opposite lost in the fields, as you might thrust a stick into the grass, tender lime leaves caressing the cheek, and silence. That is, the silence of the fields. If a breeze rustled the boughs, if a greenfinch called, if the cart-mare in the meadow shook herself, making the earth and air tremble by her with the convulsion of her mighty muscles, these were not sounds, they were the silence itself. So sensitive to it as I was, in its turn it held me firmly, like the fabled spells of old time. The mere touch of a leaf was a talisman to bring me under the enchantment, so that I seemed to feel and know all that was proceeding among the grass-blades and in the bushes. Among the lime trees along the wall the birds never built, though so close and sheltered. They built everywhere but there. To the broad coping-stones of the wall under the lime boughs speckled thrushes came almost hourly, sometimes to peer out and reconnoitre if it was safe to visit the garden, sometimes to see if a snail had climbed up the ivy. Then they dropped quietly down into the long strawberry patch immediately under. The cover of strawberries is the constant resource of all creeping things; the thrushes looked round every plant and under every leaf and runner. One toad always resided there, often two, and as you gathered a ripe strawberry you might catch sight of his black eye watching you take the fruit he had saved for you.

Down the road skims an eave-swallow, swift as an arrow, his white back making the sun-dried dust dull and dingy; he is seeking a pool for mortar, and will waver to and fro by the brook below till he finds a convenient place to alight. Thence back to the eave here, where for forty years he and his ancestors built in safety. Two white butterflies fluttering round each other rise over the limes, once more up over the house, and soar on till their white shows no longer against the illumined air. A grasshopper calls on the sward by the strawberries, and immediately fillips himself over seven leagues of grass-blades. Yonder a line of men and women file across the field, seen for a moment as they pass a gateway, and the hay changes from hay-colour to green behind them as they turn the under but still sappy side upwards. They are working hard, but it looks easy, slow, and sunny. Finches fly out from the hedgerow to the overturned hay. Another butterfly, a brown one, floats along the dusty road – the only traveller yet. The white clouds are slowly passing behind the oaks, large puffed clouds, like deliberate loads of hay, leaving little wisps and flecks behind them caught in the sky. How pleasant it would be to read in the shadow! There is a broad shadow on the sward by the strawberries cast by a tall and fine-grown American crab tree. The very place for a book; and although I know it is useless, yet I go and fetch one and dispose myself on the grass.

I can never read in summer out-of-doors. Though in shadow the bright light fills it, summer shadows are broadest daylight. The page is so white and hard, the letters so very black, the meaning and drift not quite intelligible, because neither eye nor mind will dwell upon it. Human thoughts and imaginings written down are pale and feeble in bright summer light. The eye wanders away, and rests more lovingly on greensward and green lime leaves. The mind wanders yet deeper and farther into the dreamy mystery of the azure sky. Once now and then, determined to write down that mystery and delicious sense while actually in it, I have brought out table and ink and paper, and sat there in the midst of the summer day. Three words, and where is the thought? Gone. The paper is so obviously paper, the ink so evidently ink, the pen so stiff; all so inadequate. You want colour, flexibility, light, sweet low sound – all these to paint it and play it in music, at the same time you want something that will answer to and record in one touch the strong throb of life and the thought, or feeling, or whatever it is that goes out into the earth and sky and space, endless as a beam of light.

The very shade of the pen on the paper tells you how utterly hopeless it is to express these things. There is the shade and the brilliant gleaming whiteness; now tell me in plain written words the simple contrast of the two. Not in twenty pages, for the bright light shows the paper in its common fibre-ground, coarse aspect, in its reality, not as a mind-tablet.

The delicacy and beauty of thought or feeling is so extreme that it cannot be inked in; it is like the green and blue of field and sky, of veronica flower and grass blade, which in their own existence throw light and beauty on each other, but in artificial colours repel. Take the table indoors again, and the book; the thoughts and imaginings of others are vain, and of your own too deep to be written. For the mind is filled with the exceeding beauty of these things, and their great wondrousness and marvel. Never yet have I been able to write what I felt about the sunlight only. Colour and form and light are as magic to me. It is a trance. It requires a language of ideas to convey it. It is ten years since I last reclined on that grass plot, and yet I have been writing of it as if it was yesterday, and every blade of grass is as visible and as real to me now as then. They were greener towards the house, and more brown-tinted on the margin of the strawberry bed, because towards the house the shadow rested longest. By the strawberries the fierce sunlight burned them.

The sunlight put out the books I brought into it just as it put out the fire on the hearth indoors. The tawny flames floating upwards could not bite the crackling sticks when the full beams came pouring on them. Such extravagance of light overcame the little fire till it was screened from the power of the heavens. So here in the shadow of the American crab tree the light of the sky put out the written pages. For this beautiful and wonderful light excited a sense of some likewise beautiful and wonderful truth, some unknown but grand thought hovering as a swallow above. The swallows hovered and did not alight, but they were there. An inexpressible thought quivered in the azure overhead; it could not be fully grasped, but there was a sense and feeling of its presence. Before that mere sense of its presence the weak and feeble pages, the small fires of human knowledge, dwindled and lost meaning. There was something here that was not in the books. In all the philosophies and searches of mind there was nothing that could be brought to face it, to say, This is what it intends, this is the explanation of the dream. The very grass-blades confounded the wisest, the tender lime leaf put them to shame, the grasshopper derided them, the sparrow on the wall chirped his scorn. The books were put out, unless a screen were placed between them and the light of the sky – that is, an assumption, so as to make an artificial mental darkness. Grant some assumptions – that is, screen off the light – and in that darkness everything was easily arranged, this thing here, and that yonder. But Nature grants no assumptions, and the books were put out. There is something beyond the philosophies in the light, in the grass-blades, the leaf, the grasshopper, the sparrow on the wall. Some day the great and beautiful thought which hovers on the confines of the mind will at last alight. In that is hope, the whole sky is full of abounding hope. Something beyond the books, that is consolation.

The little lawn beside the strawberry bed, burned brown there, and green towards the house shadow, holds how many myriad grass-blades? Here they are all matted together, long, and dragging each other down. Part them, and beneath them are still more, overhung and hidden. The fibres are intertangled, woven in an endless basket-work and chaos of green and dried threads. A blamable profusion this; a fifth as many would be enough; altogether a wilful waste here. As for these insects that spring out of it as I press the grass, a hundredth part of them would suffice. The American crab tree is a snowy mount in spring; the flakes of bloom, when they fall, cover the grass with a film – a bushel of bloom, which the wind takes and scatters afar. The extravagance is sublime. The two little cherry trees are as wasteful; they throw away handfuls of flower; but in the meadows the careless, spendthrift ways of grass and flower and all things are not to be expressed. Seeds by the hundred million float with absolute indifference on the air. The oak has a hundred thousand more leaves than necessary, and never hides a single acorn. Nothing utilitarian – everything on a scale of splendid waste. Such noble, broadcast, open-armed waste is delicious to behold. Never was there such a lying proverb as 'Enough is as good as a feast.' Give me the feast; give me squandered millions of seeds, luxurious carpets of petals, green mountains of oak leaves. The greater the waste, the greater the enjoyment – the nearer the approach to real life. Casuistry is of no avail; the fact is obvious; Nature flings treasures abroad, puffs them with open lips along on every breeze, piles up lavish layers of them in the free open air, packs countless numbers together in the needles of a fir tree. Prodigality and superfluity are stamped on everything she does. The ear of wheat returns a hundredfold the grain from which it grew. The surface of the earth offers to us far more than we can consume – the grains, the seeds, the fruits, the animals, the abounding products are beyond the power of all the human race to devour. They can, too, be multiplied a thousandfold. There is no natural lack. Whenever there is lack among us it is from artificial causes, which intelligence should remove.

From the littleness, and meanness, and niggardliness forced upon us by circumstances, what a relief to turn aside to the exceeding plenty of Nature! There are no bounds to it, there is no comparison to parallel it, so great is this generosity. No physical reason exists why every human being should not have sufficient, at least, of necessities. For any human being to starve, or even to be in trouble about the procuring of simple food, appears, indeed, a strange and unaccountable thing, quite upside down, and contrary to sense, if you do but consider a moment the enormous profusion the earth throws at our feet. In the slow process of time, as the human heart grows larger, such provision, I sincerely trust, will be made that no one need ever feel anxiety about mere subsistence. Then, too, let there be some imitation of this open-handed generosity and divine waste. Let the generations to come feast free of care, like my finches on the seeds of the mowing-grass, from which no voice drives them. If I could but give away as freely as the earth does!

The white-backed eave-swallow has returned many, many times from the shallow drinking-place by the brook to his half-built nest. Sometimes the pair of them cling to the mortar they have fixed under the eave, and twitter to each other about the progress of the work. They dive downwards with such velocity when they quit hold that it seems as if they must strike the ground, but they shoot up again, over the wall and the lime trees. A thrush has been to the arbour yonder twenty times; it is made of crossed laths, and overgrown with 'tea-plant', and the nest is inside the lath-work. A sparrow has visited the rose-tree by the wall – the buds are covered with aphides. A brown tree-creeper has been to the limes, then to the cherries, and even to a stout lilac stem. No matter how small the tree, he tries all that are in his way. The bright colours of a bullfinch were visible a moment just now, as he passed across the shadows farther down the garden under the damson trees and into the bushes. The grass-hopper has gone past and along the garden-path, his voice is not heard now; but there is another coming. While I have been dreaming, all these and hundreds out in the meadow have been intensely happy. So concentrated on their little work in the sunshine, so intent on the tiny egg, on the insect captured on the grass-tip to be carried to the eager fledglings, so joyful in listening to the song poured out for them or in pouring it forth, quite oblivious of all else. It is in this intense concentration that they are so happy. If they could only live longer! – but a few such seasons for them – I wish they could live a hundred years just to feast on the seeds and sing and be utterly happy and oblivious of everything but the moment they are passing. A black line has rushed up from the espalier apple yonder to the housetop thirty times at least. The starlings fly so swiftly and so straight that they seem to leave a black line along the air. They have a nest in the roof, they are to and fro it and the meadow the entire day, from dawn till eve. The espalier apple, like a screen, hides the meadow from me, so that the descending starlings appear to dive into a space behind it. Sloping downwards the meadow makes a valley; I cannot see it, but know that it is golden with buttercups, and that a brook runs in the groove of it.

Afar yonder I can see a summit beyond where the grass swells upwards to a higher level than this spot. There are bushes and elms whose height is decreased by distance on the summit, horses in the shadow of the trees, and a small flock of sheep crowded, as is their wont, in the hot and sunny gateway. By the side of the summit is a deep green trench, so it looks from here, in the hillside: it is really the course of a streamlet worn deep in the earth. I can see nothing between the top of the espalier screen and the horses under the elms on the hill. But the starlings go up and down into the hollow space, which is aglow with golden buttercups, and, indeed, I am looking over a hundred finches eagerly searching, sweetly calling, happy as the summer day. A thousand thousand grasshoppers are leaping, thrushes are labouring, filled with love and tenderness, doves cooing – there is as much joy as there are leaves on the hedges. Faster than the starling's flight my mind runs up to the streamlet in the deep green trench beside the hill.

Pleasant it was to trace it upwards, narrowing at every ascending step, till the thin stream, thinner than fragile glass, did but merely slip over the stones. A little less and it could not have run at all, water could not stretch out to greater tenuity. It smoothed the brown growth on the stones, stroking it softly. It filled up tiny basins of sand and ran out at the edges between minute rocks of flint. Beneath it went under thickest brooklime, blue flowered, and serrated water-parsnips, lost like many a mighty river for awhile among a forest of leaves. Higher up masses of bramble and projecting thorn stopped the explorer, who must wind round the grassy mound. Pausing to look back a moment there were meads under the hill with the shortest and greenest herbage, perpetually watered, and without one single buttercup, a strip of pure green among yellow flowers and yellowing corn. A few hollow oaks on whose boughs the cuckoos stayed to call, two or three peewits coursing up and down, larks singing, and for all else silence. Between the wheat and the grassy mound the path was almost closed, burdocks and brambles thrust the adventurer outward to brush against the wheat-ears. Upwards till suddenly it turned, and led by steep notches in the bank, as it seemed down to the roots of the elm trees. The clump of elms grew right over a deep and rugged hollow; their branches reached out across it, roofing in the cave.

Here was the spring, at the foot of a perpendicular rock, moss-grown low down, and overrun with creeping ivy higher. Green thorn bushes filled the chinks and made a wall to the well, and the long narrow hart's-tongue streaked the face of the cliff. Behind the thick thorns hid the course of the streamlet, in front rose the solid rock, upon the right hand the sward came to the edge – it shook every now and then as the horses in the shade of the elms stamped their feet – on the left hand the ears of wheat peered over the verge. A rocky cell in concentrated silence of green things. Now and again a finch, a starling, or a sparrow would come meaning to drink – athirst from the meadow or the cornfield – and start and almost entangle their wings in the bushes, so completely astonished that anyone should be there. The spring rises in a hollow under the rock imperceptibly, and without bubble or sound. The fine sand of the shallow basin is undisturbed – no tiny water-volcano pushes up a dome of parti-cles. Nor is there any crevice in the stone, but the basin is always full and always running over. As it slips from the brim a gleam of sunshine falls through the boughs and meets it. To this cell I used to come once now and then on a summer's day, tempted, perhaps, like the finches, by the sweet cool water, but drawn also by a feel-ing that could not be analysed. Stooping, I lifted the water in the hollow of my hand – carefully, lest the sand might be disturbed – and the sunlight gleamed on it as it slipped through ray fingers. Alone in the green-roofed cave, alone with the sunlight and the pure water, there was a sense of something more than these. The water was more to me than water, and the sun than sun. The gleaming rays on the water in my palm held me for a moment, the touch of the water gave me something from itself. A moment, and the gleam was gone, the water flowing away, but I had had them. Beside the physical water and physical light I had received from them their beauty; they had communicated to me this silent mystery. The pure and beautiful water, the pure, clear, and beau-tiful light, each had given me something of their truth.

So many times I came to it, toiling up the long and shadowless bill in the burning sunshine, often carrying a vessel to take some of it home with me. There was a brook, indeed but this was different, it was the spring; it was taken home as a beautiful flower might be brought. It is not the physical water, it is the sense or feeling that it conveys. Nor is it the physical sunshine; it is the sense of inexpressible beauty which it brings with it. Of such I still drink, and hope to do so still deeper.

Gloire de Dijon

D. H. LAWRENCE

When she rises in the morning
I linger to watch her;
She spreads the bath-cloth underneath the
   window
And the sunbeams catch her
Glistening white on the shoulders,
While down her sides the mellow
Golden shadow glows as
She stoops to the sponge, and her swung breasts
Sway like full-blown yellow
Gloire de Dijon roses.

She drips herself with water, and her shoulders
Glisten as silver, they crumple up
Like wet and falling roses, and I listen
For the sluicing of their rain-dishevelled petals.
In the window full of sunlight
Concentrates her golden shadow
Fold on fold, until it glows as
Mellow as the glory roses.

The Secret Garden *(excerpt)*

FRANCES HODGSON BURNETT

CHAPTER X

Dickon

The sun shone down for nearly a week on the secret garden. The Secret Garden was what Mary called it when she was thinking of it. She liked the name, and she liked still more the feeling that when its beautiful old walls shut her in no one knew where she was. It seemed almost like being shut out of the world in some fairy place. The few books she had read and liked had been fairy-story books, and she had read of secret gardens in some of the stories. Sometimes people went to sleep in them for a hundred years, which she had thought must be rather stupid. She had no intention of going to sleep, and, in fact, she was becoming wider awake every day which passed at Misselthwaite. She was beginning to like to be out of doors; she no longer hated the wind, but enjoyed it. She could run faster, and longer, and she could skip up to a hundred. The bulbs in the secret garden must have been much astonished. Such nice clear places were made round them that they had all the breathing space they wanted, and really, if Mistress Mary had known it, they began to cheer up under the dark earth and work tremendously. The sun could get at them and warm them, and when the rain came down it could reach them at once, so they began to feel very much alive.

Mary was an odd, determined little person, and now she had something interesting to be determined about, she was very much absorbed, indeed. She worked and dug and pulled up weeds steadily, only becoming more pleased with her work every hour instead of tiring of it. It seemed to her like a fascinating sort of play. She found many more of the sprouting pale green points than she had ever hoped to find. They seemed to be starting up everywhere and each day she was sure she found tiny new ones, some so tiny that they barely peeped above the earth. There were so many that she remembered what Martha had said about the 'snowdrops by the thousands', and about bulbs spreading and making new ones. These had been left to themselves for ten years and perhaps they had spread, like the snowdrops, into thousands. She wondered how long it would be before they showed that they were flowers. Sometimes she stopped digging to look at the garden and try to imagine what it would be like when it was covered with thousands of lovely things in bloom. During that week of sunshine, she became more intimate with Ben Weatherstaff. She surprised him several times by seeming to start up beside him as if she sprang out of the earth. The truth was that she was afraid that he would pick up his tools and go away if he saw her coming, so she always walked toward him as silently as possible. But, in fact, he did not object to her as strongly as he had at first. Perhaps he was secretly rather flattered by her evident desire for his elderly company. Then, also, she was more civil than she had been. He did not know that when she first saw him she spoke to him as she would have spoken to a native, and had not known that a cross, sturdy old Yorkshire man was not accustomed to salaam to his masters, and be merely commanded by them to do things.

'Tha'rt like th' robin,' he said to her one morning when he lifted his head and saw her standing by him. 'I never knows when I shall see thee or which side tha'll come from.'

'He's friends with me now,' said Mary.

'That's like him,' snapped Ben Weatherstaff. 'Makin' up to th' women folk just for vanity an' flightiness. There's nothin' he wouldn't do for th' sake o' showin' off an' flirtin' his tail-feathers. He's as full o' pride as an egg's full o' meat.'

He very seldom talked much and sometimes did not even answer Mary's questions except by a grunt, but this morning he said more than usual. He stood up and rested one hobnailed boot on the top of his spade while he looked her over.

'How long has tha' been here?' he jerked out.

'I think it's about a month,' she answered.

'Tha's beginnin' to do Misselthwaite credit,' he said. 'Tha's a bit fatter than tha' was an' tha's not quite so yeller. Tha' looked like a young plucked crow when tha' first came into this garden. Thinks I to myself I never set eyes on an uglier, sourer faced young 'un.'

Mary was not vain and as she had never thought much of her looks she was not greatly disturbed.

'I know I'm fatter,' she said. 'My stockings are getting tighter. They used to make wrinkles. There's the robin, Ben Weatherstaff.'

There, indeed, was the robin, and she thought he looked nicer than ever. His red waistcoat was as glossy as satin and he flirted his wings and tail and tilted his head and hopped about with all sorts of lively graces. He seemed determined to make Ben Weatherstaff admire him. But Ben was sarcastic.

'Aye, there tha' art!' he said. 'Tha' can put up with me for a bit sometimes when tha's got no one better. Tha's been reddenin' up thy waistcoat an' polishin' thy feathers this two weeks. I know what tha's up to. Tha's courtin' some bold young madam somewhere tellin' thy lies to her about bein' th' finest cock robin on Missel Moor an' ready to fight all th' rest of 'em.'

'Oh! look at him!' exclaimed Mary.

The robin was evidently in a fascinating, bold mood. He hopped closer and closer and looked at Ben Weatherstaff more and more engagingly. He flew on to the nearest currant bush and tilted his head and sang a little song right at him.

'Tha' thinks tha'll get over me by doin' that,' said Ben, wrinkling his face up in such a way that Mary felt sure he was trying not to look pleased. 'Tha' thinks no one can stand out against thee – that's what tha' thinks.'

The robin spread his wings – Mary could scarcely believe her eyes. He flew right up to the handle of Ben Weatherstaff's spade and alighted on the top of it. Then the old man's face wrinkled itself slowly into a new expression. He stood still as if he were afraid to breathe – as if he would not have stirred for the world, lest his robin should start away. He spoke quite in a whisper.

'Well, I'm danged!' he said as softly as if he were saying something quite different. 'Tha' does know how to get at a chap – tha' does! Tha's fair unearthly, tha's so knowin'.'

And he stood without stirring – almost without drawing his breath – until the robin gave another flirt to his wings and flew away. Then he stood looking at the handle of the spade as if there might be Magic in it, and then he began to dig again and said nothing for several minutes.

But because he kept breaking into a slow grin now and then, Mary was not afraid to talk to him.

'Have you a garden of your own?' she asked.

'No. I'm bachelder an' lodge with Martin at th' gate.'

'If you had one,' said Mary, 'what would you plant?'

'Cabbages an' 'taters an' onions.'

'But if you wanted to make a flower garden,' persisted Mary, 'what would you plant?'

'Bulbs an' sweet-smellin' things – but mostly roses.'

Mary's face lighted up.

'Do you like roses?' she said.

Ben Weatherstaff rooted up a weed and threw it aside before he answered.

'Well, yes, I do. I was learned that by a young lady I was gardener to. She had a lot in a place she was fond of, an' she loved 'em like they was children – or robins. I've seen her bend over an' kiss 'em.' He dragged out another weed and scowled at it. 'That were as much as ten year' ago.'

'Where is she now?' asked Mary, much interested.

230

'Heaven,' he answered, and drove his spade deep into the soil, ''cording to what parson says.'

'What happened to the roses?' Mary asked again, more interested than ever.

'They was left to themselves.'

Mary was becoming quite excited.

'Did they quite die? Do roses quite die when they are left to themselves?' she ventured.

'Well, I'd got to like 'em – an' I liked her – an' she liked 'em,' Ben Weatherstaff admitted reluctantly. 'Once or twice a year I'd go an' work at 'em a bit – prune 'em an' dig about th' roots. They run wild, but they was in rich soil, so some of 'em lived.'

'When they have no leaves and look grey and brown and dry, how can you tell whether they are dead or alive?' inquired Mary.

'Wait till th' spring gets at 'em – wait till th' sun shines on th' rain and th' rain falls on th' sunshine an' then tha'll find out.'

'How – how?' cried Mary, forgetting to be careful. 'Look along th' twigs an' branches an' if tha' see a bit of a brown lump swelling here an' there, watch it after th' warm rain an' see what happens.' He stopped suddenly and looked curiously at her eager face. 'Why does tha' care so much about roses an' such, all of a sudden?' he demanded.

Mistress Mary felt her face grow red. She was almost afraid to answer.

'I – I want to play that – that I have a garden of my own,' she stammered. 'I – there is nothing for me to do. I have nothing – and no one.'

'Well,' said Ben Weatherstaff slowly, as he watched her, 'that's true. Tha' hasn't.'

He said it in such an odd way that Mary wondered if he was actually a little sorry for her. She had never felt sorry for herself; she had only felt tired and cross, because she disliked people and things so much. But now the world seemed to be changing and getting nicer. If no one found out about the secret garden, she should enjoy herself always.

She stayed with him for ten or fifteen minutes longer and asked him as many questions as she dared. He answered every one of them in his queer grunting way and he did not seem really cross and did not pick up his spade and leave her. He said something about roses just as she was going away and it reminded her of the ones he had said he had been fond of.

'Do you go and see those other roses now?' she asked.

'Not been this year. My rheumatics has made me too stiff in th' joints.'

He said it in his grumbling voice, and then quite suddenly he seemed to get angry with her, though she did not see why he should.

'Now look here!' he said sharply. 'Don't tha' ask so many questions. Tha'rt th' worst wench for askin' questions I've ever come across. Get thee gone an' play thee. I've done talkin' for today.'

And he said it so crossly that she knew there was not the least use in staying another minute. She went skipping slowly down the outside walk, thinking him over and saying to herself that, queer as it was, here was another person whom she liked in spite of his crossness. She liked old Ben Weatherstaff. Yes, she did like him. She always wanted to try to make him talk to her. Also she began to believe that he knew everything in the world about flowers.

There was a laurel-hedged walk which curved round the secret garden and ended at a gate which opened into a wood, in the park. She thought she would slip round this walk and look into the wood and see if there were any rabbits hopping about. She enjoyed the skipping very much and when she reached the little gate she opened it and went through because she heard a low, peculiar whistling sound and wanted to find out what it was.

It was a very strange thing indeed. She quite caught her breath as she stopped to look at it. A boy was sitting under a tree, with his back against it, playing on a rough wooden pipe. He was a funny looking boy about twelve. He looked very clean and his nose turned up and his cheeks were as red as poppies and never had Mistress Mary seen such round and such blue eyes in any boy's face. And on the trunk of the tree he leaned against, a brown squirrel was clinging and watching him, and from behind a bush nearby a cock pheasant was delicately stretching his neck to peep out, and quite near him were two rabbits sitting up and sniffing with tremulous noses – and actually it appeared as if they were all drawing near to watch him and listen to the strange low little call his pipe seemed to make.

When he saw Mary he held up his hand and spoke to her in a voice almost as low as and rather like his piping.

'Don't tha' move,' he said. 'It'd flight 'em.' Mary remained motionless. He stopped playing his pipe and began to rise from the ground. He moved so slowly that it scarcely seemed as though he were moving at all, but at last he stood on his feet and then the squirrel scampered back up into the branches of his tree, the pheasant withdrew his head and the rabbits dropped on all fours and began to hop away, though not at all as if they were frightened.

'I'm Dickon,' the boy said. 'I know tha'rt Miss Mary.'

Then Mary realised that somehow she had known at first that he was Dickon. Who else could have been charming rabbits and pheasants as the natives charm snakes in India? He had a wide, red, curving mouth and his smile spread all over his face.

'I got up slow,' he explained, 'because if tha' makes a quick move it startles 'em. A body 'as to move gentle an' speak low when wild things is about.'

He did not speak to her as if they had never seen each other before but as if he knew her quite well. Mary knew nothing about boys and she spoke to him a little stiffly because she felt rather shy.

'Did you get Martha's letter?' she asked.

He nodded his curly, rust-coloured head. 'That's why I come.'

He stooped to pick up something which had been lying on the ground beside him when he piped.

'I've got th' garden tools. There's a little spade an' rake an' a fork an' hoe. Eh! they are good 'uns. There's a trowel, too. An' th' woman in th' shop threw in a packet o' white poppy an' one o' blue larkspur when I bought th' other seeds.'

'Will you show the seeds to me?' Mary said.

She wished she could talk as he did. His speech was so quick and easy. It sounded as if he liked her and was not the least afraid she would not like him, though he was only a common moor boy, in patched clothes and with a funny face and a rough, rusty-red head. As she came closer to him she noticed that there was a clean fresh scent of heather and grass and leaves about him, almost as if he were made of them. She liked it very much and when she looked into his funny face with the red cheeks and round blue eyes she forgot that she had felt shy.

'Let us sit down on this log and look at them,' she said.

They sat down and he took a clumsy little brown paper package out of his coat pocket. He untied the string and inside there were ever so many neater and smaller packages with a picture of a flower on each one.

'There's a lot o' mignonette an' poppies,' he said. 'Mignonette's th' sweetest smellin' thing as grows, an' it'll grow wherever you cast it, same as poppies will. Them as'll come up an' bloom if you just whistle to 'em, them's th' nicest of all.' He stopped and turned his head quickly, his poppy-cheeked face lighting up.

'Where's that robin as is callin' us?' he said.

The chirp came from a thick holly bush, bright with scarlet berries, and Mary thought she knew whose it was.

'Is it really calling us?' she asked.

'Aye,' said Dickon, as if it was the most natural thing in the world, 'he's callin' someone he's friends with. That's same as sayin' "Here I am. Look at me. I wants a bit of a chat." There he is in the bush. Whose is he?'

'He's Ben Weatherstaff's, but I think he knows me a little,' answered Mary.

'Aye, he knows thee,' said Dickon in his low voice again. 'An' he likes thee. He's took thee on. He'll tell me all about thee in a minute.'

He moved quite close to the bush with the slow movement Mary had noticed before, and then he made a sound almost like the robin's own twitter. The robin listened a few seconds, intently, and then answered quite as if he were replying to a question.

'Aye, he's a friend o' yours,' chuckled Dickon.

'Do you think he is?' cried Mary eagerly. She did so want to know. 'Do you think he really likes me?'

'He wouldn't come near thee if he didn't,' answered Dickon. 'Birds is rare choosers an' a robin can flout a body worse than a man. See, he's making up to thee now. "Cannot tha' see a chap?" he's sayin'.'

And it really seemed as if it must be true. He so sidled and twittered and tilted as he hopped on his bush.

'Do you understand everything birds say?' said Mary.

Dickon's grin spread until he seemed all wide, red, curving mouth, and he rubbed his rough head.

'I think I do, and they think I do,' he said. 'I've lived on th' moor with 'em so long. I've watched 'em break shell an' come out an' fledge an' learn to fly an' begin to sing, till I think I'm one of 'em. Sometimes I think p'raps I'm a bird, or a fox, or a rabbit, or a squirrel, or even a beetle, an' I don't know it.'

He laughed and came back to the log and began to talk about the flower seeds again. He told her what they looked like when they were flowers; he told her how to plant them, and watch them, and feed and water them.

'See here,' he said suddenly, turning round to look at her. 'I'll plant them for thee myself. Where is tha' garden?'

Mary's thin hands clutched each other as they lay on her lap. She did not know what to say, so for a whole minute she said nothing. She had never thought of this. She felt miserable. And she felt as if she went red and then pale.

'Tha's got a bit o' garden, hasn't tha'?' Dickon said.

It was true that she had turned red and then pale. Dickon saw her do it, and as she still said nothing, he began to be puzzled.

'Wouldn't they give thee a bit?' he asked. 'Hasn't tha' got any yet?'

She held her hands tighter and turned her eyes toward him.

'I don't know anything about boys,' she said slowly. 'Could you keep a secret, if I told you one? It's a great secret. I don't know what I should do if anyone found it out. I believe I should die!' She said the last sentence quite fiercely.

Dickon looked more puzzled than ever and even rubbed his hand over his rough head again, but he answered quite good-humouredly. 'I'm keepin' secrets all th' time,' he said. 'If I couldn't keep secrets from th' other lads, secrets about foxes' cubs, an' birds' nests, an' wild things' holes, there'd be naught safe on th' moor. Aye, I can keep secrets.'

Mistress Mary did not mean to put out her hand and clutch his sleeve but she did it.

'I've stolen a garden,' she said very fast. 'It isn't mine. It isn't anybody's. Nobody wants it, nobody cares for it, nobody ever goes into it. Perhaps everything is dead in it already. I don't know.'

She began to feel hot and as contrary as she had ever felt in her life.

'I don't care, I don't care! Nobody has any right to take it from me when I care about it and they don't. They're letting it die, all shut in by itself,' she ended passionately, and she threw her arms over her face and burst out crying – poor little Mistress Mary.

Dickon's curious blue eyes grew rounder and rounder. 'Eh-h-h!' he said, drawing his exclamation out slowly, and the way he did it meant both wonder and sympathy.

'I've nothing to do,' said Mary. 'Nothing belongs to me. I found it myself and I got into it myself. I was only just like the robin, and they wouldn't take it from the robin.'

'Where is it?' asked Dickon in a dropped voice.

Mistress Mary got up from the log at once. She knew she felt contrary again, and obstinate, and she did not care at all. She was imperious and Indian, and at the same time hot and sorrowful.

'Come with me and I'll show you,' she said.

She led him round the laurel path and to the walk where the ivy grew so thickly. Dickon followed her with a queer, almost pitying, look on his face. He felt as if he were being led to look at some strange bird's nest and must move softly. When she stepped to the wall and lifted the hanging ivy he started. There was a door and Mary pushed it slowly open and they passed in together, and then Mary stood and waved her hand round defiantly.

'It's this,' she said. 'It's a secret garden, and I'm the only one in the world who wants it to be alive.'

Dickon looked round and round about it, and round and round again.

'Eh!' he almost whispered, 'it is a queer, pretty place! It's like as if a body was in a dream.'

CHAPTER XI

The Nest of the Missel Thrush

For two or three minutes he stood looking round him, while Mary watched him, and then he began to walk about softly, even more lightly than Mary had walked the first time she had found herself inside the four walls. His eyes seemed to be taking in everything – the grey trees with the grey creepers climbing over them and hanging from their branches, the tangle on the walls and among the grass, the evergreen alcoves with the stone seats and tall flower urns standing in them.

'I never thought I'd see this place,' he said at last, in a whisper.

'Did you know about it?' asked Mary.

She had spoken aloud and he made a sign to her.

'We must talk low,' he said, 'or someone'll hear us an' wonder what's to do in here.'

'Oh! I forgot!' said Mary, feeling frightened and putting her hand quickly against her mouth. 'Did you know about the garden?' she asked again when she had recovered herself. Dickon nodded.

'Martha told me there was one as no one ever went inside,' he answered. 'Us used to wonder what it was like.'

He stopped and looked round at the lovely grey tangle about him, and his round eyes looked queerly happy.

'Eh! the nests as'll be here come springtime,' he said. 'It'd be th' safest nestin' place in England. No one never comin' near an' tangles o' trees an' roses to build in. I wonder all th' birds on th' moor don't build here.'

Mistress Mary put her hand on his arm again without knowing it.

'Will there be roses?' she whispered. 'Can you tell? I thought perhaps they were all dead.'

'Eh! No! Not them – not all of 'em!' he answered. 'Look here!'

He stepped over to the nearest tree – an old, old one with grey lichen all over its bark, but upholding a curtain of tangled sprays and branches. He took a thick knife out of his pocket and opened one of its blades.

'There's lots o' dead wood as ought to be cut out,' he said. 'An' there's a lot o' old wood, but it made some new last year. This here's a new bit,' and he touched a shoot which looked brownish green instead of hard, dry grey. Mary touched it herself in an eager, reverent way.

'That one?' she said. 'Is that one quite alive – quite?'

Dickon curved his wide smiling mouth.

'It's as wick as you or me,' he said; and Mary remembered that Martha had told her that 'wick' meant 'alive' or 'lively'.

'I'm glad it's wick!' she cried out in her whisper. 'I want them all to be wick. Let us go round the garden and count how many wick ones there are.'

She quite panted with eagerness, and Dickon was as eager as she was. They went from tree to tree and from bush to bush. Dickon carried his knife in his hand and showed her things which she thought wonderful.

'They've run wild,' he said, 'but th' strongest ones has fair thrived on it. The delicatest ones has died out, but th' others has growed an' growed, an' spread an' spread, till they's a wonder.

See here!' and he pulled down a thick grey, dry-looking branch. 'A body might think this was dead wood, but I don't believe it is – down to th' root. I'll cut it low down an' see.'

He knelt and with his knife cut the lifeless-looking branch through, not far above the earth.

'There!' he said exultantly. 'I told thee so. There's green in that wood yet. Look at it.'

Mary was down on her knees before he spoke, gazing with all her might.

'When it looks a bit greenish an' juicy like that, it's wick,' he explained. 'When th' inside is dry an' breaks easy, like this here piece I've cut off, it's done for. There's a big root here as all this live wood sprung out of, an' if th' old wood's cut off an' it's dug round, and took care of there'll be—' he stopped and lifted his face to look up at the climbing and hanging sprays above him – 'there'll be a fountain o' roses here this summer.'

They went from bush to bush and from tree to tree. He was very strong and clever with his knife and knew how to cut the dry and dead wood away, and could tell when an unpromising bough or twig had still green life in it. In the course of half an hour Mary thought she could tell too, and when he cut through a lifeless-looking branch she would cry out joyfully under her breath when she caught sight of the least shade of moist green. The spade, and hoe, and fork were very useful. He showed her how to use the fork while he dug about roots with the spade and stirred the earth and let the air in.

They were working industriously round one of the biggest standard roses when he caught sight of something which made him utter an exclamation of surprise.

'Why!' he cried, pointing to the grass a few feet away. 'Who did that there?'

It was one of Mary's own little clearings round the pale green points.

'I did it,' said Mary.

'Why, I thought tha' didn't know nothin' about gardenin',' he exclaimed.

'I don't,' she answered, 'but they were so little, and the grass was so thick and strong, and they looked as if they had no room to breathe. So I made a place for them. I don't even know what they are.'

Dickon went and knelt down by them, smiling his wide smile.

'Tha' was right,' he said. 'A gardener couldn't have told thee better. They'll grow now like Jack's bean-stalk. They're crocuses an' snowdrops, an' these here is narcissuses,' turning to another patch, 'an here's daffydowndillys. Eh! they will be a sight.'

He ran from one clearing to another.

'Tha' has done a lot o' work for such a little wench,' he said, looking her over.

'I'm growing fatter,' said Mary, 'and I'm growing stronger. I used always to be tired. When I dig I'm not tired at all. I like to smell the earth when it's turned up.'

'It's rare good for thee,' he said, nodding his head wisely. 'There's naught as nice as th' smell o' good clean earth, except th' smell o' fresh growin' things when th' rain falls on 'em. I get out on th' moor many a day when it's rainin' an' I lie under a bush an' listen to th' soft swish o' drops on th' heather an' I just sniff an' sniff. My nose end fair quivers like a rabbit's, mother says.'

'Do you never catch cold?' inquired Mary, gazing at him wonderingly. She had never seen such a funny boy, or such a nice one.

'Not me,' he said, grinning. 'I never ketched cold since I was born. I wasn't brought up nesh enough. I've chased about th' moor in all weathers same as th' rabbits does. Mother says I've sniffed up too much fresh air for twelve year' to ever get to sniffin' with cold. I'm as tough as a white-thorn knobstick.'

He was working all the time he was talking and Mary was following him and helping him with her fork or the trowel.

'There's a lot of work to do here!' he said once, looking about quite exultantly.

'Will you come again and help me to do it?' Mary begged. 'I'm sure I can help, too. I can dig and pull up weeds, and do whatever you tell me. Oh! do come, Dickon!'

'I'll come every day if tha' wants me, rain or shine,' he answered stoutly. 'It's the best fun I ever had in my life – shut in here an' wakenin' up a garden.'

'If you will come,' said Mary, 'if you will help me to make it alive I'll – I don't know what I'll do,' she ended helplessly. What could you do for a boy like that?

'I'll tell thee what tha'll do,' said Dickon, with his happy grin. 'Tha'll get fat an' tha'll get as hungry as a young fox an' tha'll learn how to talk to th' robin same as I do. Eh! we'll have a lot o' fun.'

He began to walk about, looking up in the trees and at the walls and bushes with a thoughtful expression.

'I wouldn't want to make it look like a gardener's garden, all clipped an' spick an' span, would you?' he said. 'It's nicer like this with things runnin' wild, an' swingin' an' catchin' hold of each other.'

'Don't let us make it tidy,' said Mary anxiously. 'It wouldn't seem like a secret garden if it was tidy.'

Dickon stood rubbing his rusty-red head with a rather puzzled look. 'It's a secret garden sure enough,' he said, 'but seems like someone besides th' robin must have been in it since it was shut up ten year' ago.'

'But the door was locked and the key was buried,' said Mary. 'No one could get in.'

'That's true,' he answered. 'It's a queer place. Seems to me as if there'd been a bit o' prunin' done here an' there, later than ten year' ago.'

'But how could it have been done?' said Mary.

He was examining a branch of a standard rose and he shook his head.

'Aye! how could it!' he murmured. 'With th' door locked an' th' key buried.'

Mistress Mary always felt that however many years she lived she should never forget that first morning when her garden began to grow. Of course, it did seem to begin to grow for her that morning. When Dickon began to clear places to plant seeds, she remembered what Basil had sung at her when he wanted to tease her.

'Are there any flowers that look like bells?' she inquired.

'Lilies o' th' valley does,' he answered, digging away with the trowel, 'an' there's Canterbury bells, an' campanulas.'

'Let's plant some,' said Mary.

'There's lilies o' th' valley here already; I saw 'em. They'll have growed too close an' we'll have to separate 'em, but there's plenty. Th' other ones takes two years to bloom from seed, but I can bring you some bits o' plants from our cottage garden. Why does tha' want 'em?'

Then Mary told him about Basil and his brothers and sisters in India and of how she had hated them and of their calling her 'Mistress Mary Quite Contrary'.

'They used to dance round and sing at me. They sang—
"Mistress Mary, quite contrary,
How does your garden grow?
With silver bells, and cockle shells,
And marigolds all in a row."
I just remembered it and it made me wonder if there were really flowers like silver bells.'

She frowned a little and gave her trowel a rather spiteful dig into the earth.

'I wasn't as contrary as they were.'

But Dickon laughed.

'Eh!' he said, and as he crumbled the rich black soil she saw he was sniffing up the scent of it. 'There doesn't seem to be no need for no one to be contrary when there's flowers an' such like, an' such lots o' friendly wild things runnin' about makin' homes for themselves, or buildin' nests an' singin' an' whistlin', does there?'

Mary, kneeling by him holding the seeds, looked at him and stopped frowning.

'Dickon,' she said, 'you are as nice as Martha said you were. I like you, and you make the fifth person. I never thought I should like five people.'

Dickon sat up on his heels as Martha did when she was polishing the grate. He did look funny and delightful, Mary thought, with his round blue eyes and red cheeks and happy looking turned-up nose.

'Only five folk as tha' likes?' he said. 'Who is th' other four?'

'Your mother and Martha,' Mary checked them off on her fingers, 'and the robin and Ben Weatherstaff.'

Dickon laughed so that he was obliged to stifle the sound by putting his arm over his mouth.

'I know tha' thinks I'm a queer lad,' he said, 'but I think tha' art th' queerest little lass I ever saw.'

Then Mary did a strange thing. She leaned forward and asked him a question she had never dreamed of asking anyone before. And she tried to ask it in Yorkshire because that was his language, and in India a native was always pleased if you knew his speech.

'Does tha' like me?' she said.

'Eh!' he answered heartily, 'that I does. I likes thee wonderful, an' so does th' robin, I do believe!'

'That's two, then,' said Mary. 'That's two for me.'

And then they began to work harder than ever and more joyfully. Mary was startled and sorry when she heard the big clock in the courtyard strike the hour of her midday dinner.

'I shall have to go,' she said mournfully. 'And you will have to go too, won't you?'

Dickon grinned.

'My dinner's easy to carry about with me,' he said. 'Mother always lets me put a bit o' somethin' in my pocket.'

He picked up his coat from the grass and brought out of a pocket a lumpy little bundle tied up in a quite clean, coarse, blue and white handkerchief. It held two thick pieces of bread with a slice of something laid between them.

'It's oftenest naught but bread,' he said, 'but I've got a fine slice o' fat bacon with it today.'

Mary thought it looked a queer dinner, but he seemed ready to enjoy it.

'Run on an' get thy victuals,' he said. 'I'll be done with mine first. I'll get some more work done before I start back home.'

He sat down with his back against a tree.

'I'll call th' robin up,' he said, 'and give him th' rind o' th' bacon to peck at. They likes a bit o' fat wonderful.'

Mary could scarcely bear to leave him. Suddenly it seemed as if he might be a sort of wood fairy who might be gone when she came into the garden again. He seemed too good to be true. She went slowly half-way to the door in the wall and then she stopped and went back.

'Whatever happens, you – you never would tell?' she said.

His poppy-coloured cheeks were distended with his first big bite of bread and bacon, but he managed to smile encouragingly.

'If tha' was a missel thrush an' showed me where thy nest was, does tha' think I'd tell anyone? Not me,' he said. 'Tha' art as safe as a missel thrush.'

And she was quite sure she was.

The Spinner and the Monks *(excerpt)*

D. H. LAWRENCE

The schoolmistress had told me I should find snowdrops behind San Tommaso. If she had not asserted such confident knowledge I should have doubted her translation of *perceneige*. She meant Christmas roses all the while.

However, I went looking for snowdrops. The walls broke down suddenly, and I was out in a grassy olive orchard, following a track beside pieces of fallen overgrown masonry. So I came to skirt the brink of a steep little gorge, at the bottom of which a stream was rushing down its steep slant to the lake. Here I stood to look for my snowdrops. The grassy, rocky bank went down steep from my feet. I heard water tittle-tattling away in deep shadow below. There were pale flecks in the dimness, but these, I knew, were primroses. So I scrambled down.

Looking up, out of the heavy shadow that lay in the cleft, I could see, right in the sky, grey rocks shining transcendent in the pure empyrean. 'Are they so far up?' I thought. I did not dare to say, 'Am I so far down?' But I was uneasy. Nevertheless it was a lovely place, in the cold shadow, complete; when one forgot the shining rocks far above, it was a complete, shadowless world of shadow. Primroses were everywhere in nests of pale bloom upon the dark, steep face of the cleft, and tongues of fern hanging out, and here and there under the rods and twigs of bushes were tufts of wrecked Christmas roses, nearly over, but still, in the coldest corners, the lovely buds like handfuls of snow. There had been such crowded sumptuous tufts of Christmas roses everywhere in the stream-gullies, during the shadow of winter, that these few remaining flowers were hardly noticeable.

I gathered instead the primroses, that smelled of earth and of the weather. There were no snowdrops. I had found the day before a bank of crocuses, pale, fragile, lilac-coloured flowers with dark veins, pricking up keenly like myriad little lilac-coloured flames among the grass, under the olive trees. And I wanted very much to find the snowdrops hanging in the gloom. But there were not any.

I gathered a handful of primroses, then I climbed suddenly, quickly out of the deep watercourse, anxious to get back to the sunshine before the evening fell. Up above I saw the olive trees in the sunny golden grass, and sunlit grey rocks immensely high up. I was afraid lest the evening would fall whilst I was groping about like an otter in the damp and the darkness, that the day of sunshine would be over.

Soon I was up in the sunshine again, on the turf under the olive trees, reassured. It was the upper world of glowing light, and I was safe again.

All the olives were gathered, and the mills were going night and day, making a great, acrid scent of olive oil in preparation, by the lake. The little stream rattled down. A mule driver 'Hued!' to his mules on the Strada Vecchia. High up, on the Strada Nuova, the beautiful, new, military high-road, which winds with beautiful curves up the mountain-side, crossing the same stream several times in clear-leaping bridges, travelling cut out of sheer slope high above the lake, winding beautifully and gracefully forward to the Austrian frontier, where it ends: high up on the lovely swinging road, in the strong evening sunshine, I saw a bullock wagon moving like a vision, though the clanking of the wagon and the crack of the bullock whip responded close in my ears.

Everything was clear and sun-coloured up there, clear-grey rocks partaking of the sky, tawny grass and scrub, browny-green spires of cypresses, and then the mist of grey-green olives fuming down to the lake-side. There was no shadow, only clear sun-substance built up to the sky, a bullock wagon moving slowly in the high sunlight, along the uppermost terrace of the military road. It sat in the warm stillness of the transcendent afternoon.

The four o'clock steamer was creeping down the lake from the Austrian end, creeping under the cliffs. Far away, the Verona side, beyond the Island, lay fused in dim gold. The mountain opposite was so still, that my heart seemed to fade in its beating as if it too would be still. All was perfectly still, pure substance. The little steamer on the floor of the world below, the mules down the road cast no shadow. They too were pure sun-substance travelling on the surface of the sun-made world.

A cricket hopped near me. Then I remembered that it was Saturday afternoon, when a strange suspension comes over the world. And then, just below me, I saw two monks walking in their garden between the naked, bony vines, walking in their wintry garden of bony vines and olive trees, their brown cassocks passing between the brown vine-stocks, their heads bare to the sunshine, sometimes a glint of light as their feet strode from under their skirts.

It was so still, everything so perfectly suspended, that I felt them talking. They marched with the peculiar march of monks, a long, loping stride, their heads together, their skirts swaying slowly, two brown monks with hidden hands, sliding under the bony vines and beside the cabbages, their heads always together in hidden converse. It was as if I were attending with my dark soul to their inaudible undertone. All the time I sat still in silence, I was one with them, a partaker, though I could hear no sound of their voices. I went with the long stride of their skirted feet, that slid springless and noiseless from end to end of the garden, and back again. Their hands were kept down at their sides, hidden in the long sleeves, and the skirts of their robes. They did not touch each other, nor gesticulate as they walked. There was no motion save the long, furtive stride and the heads leaning together. Yet there was an eagerness in their conversation. Almost like shadow-creatures ventured out of their cold, obscure element, they went backwards and forwards in their wintry garden, thinking nobody could see them.

Across, above them, was the faint, rousing dazzle of snow. They never looked up. But the dazzle of snow began to glow as they walked, the wonderful, faint, ethereal flush of the long range of snow in the heavens, at evening, began to kindle.

Another world was coming to pass, the cold, rare night. It was dawning in exquisite, icy rose upon the long mountain-summit opposite. The monks walked backwards and forwards, talking, in the first undershadow.

And I noticed that up above the snow, frail in the bluish sky, a frail moon had put forth, like a thin, scalloped film of ice floated out on the slow current of the coming night. And a bell sounded.

And still the monks were pacing backwards and forwards, backwards and forwards, with a strange, neutral regularity.

The shadows were coming across everything, because of the mountains in the west. Already the olive wood where I sat was extinguished. This was the world of the monks, the rim of pallor between night and day. Here they paced, backwards and forwards, backwards and forwards, in the neutral, shadowless light of shadow.

Neither the flare of day nor the completeness of night reached them, they paced the narrow path of the twilight, treading in the neutrality of the law. Neither the blood nor the spirit spoke in them, only the law, the abstraction of the average. The infinite is positive and negative. But the average is only neutral. And the monks trod backward and forward down the line of neutrality.

Meanwhile, on the length of mountain-ridge, the snow grew rosy-incandescent, like heaven breaking into blossom. After all, eternal not-being and eternal being are the same. In the rosy snow that shone in heaven over a darkened earth was the ecstasy of consummation. Night and day are one, light and dark are one, both the same in the origin and in the issue, both the same in the moment, of ecstasy, light fused in darkness and darkness fused in light, as in the rosy snow above the twilight.

But in the monks it was not ecstasy, in them it was neutrality, the under earth. Transcendent, above the shadowed, twilit earth was the rosy snow of ecstasy. But spreading far over us, down below, was the neutrality of the twilight, of the monks. The flesh neutralising the spirit, the spirit neutralising the flesh, the law of the average asserted, this was the monks as they paced backward and forward.

The moon climbed higher, away from the snowy, fading ridge, she became gradually herself. Between the roots of the olive tree was a rosy-tipped daisy just going to sleep. I gathered it and put it among the frail, moony little bunch of primroses, so that its sleep should warm the rest. Also I put in some little periwinkles, that were very blue, reminding me of the eyes of the old woman.

The day was gone, the twilight was gone, and the snow was invisible as I came down to the side of the lake. Only the moon, white and shining, was in the sky, like a woman glorying in her own loveliness as she loiters superbly to the gaze of all the world, looking sometimes through the fringe of dark olive leaves, sometimes looking at her own superb, quivering body, wholly naked in the water of the lake.

My little old woman was gone. She, all day-sunshine, would have none of the moon. Always she must live like a bird, looking down on all the world at once, so that it lay all subsidiary to herself, herself the wakeful consciousness hovering over the world like a hawk, like a sleep of wakefulness. And, like a bird, she went to sleep as the shadows came.

She did not know the yielding up of the senses and the possession of the unknown, through the senses, which happens under a superb moon. The all-glorious sun knows none of these yieldings up. He takes his way. And the daisies at once go to sleep. And the soul of the old spinning-woman also closed up at sunset, the rest was a sleep, a cessation.

It is all so strange and varied: the dark-skinned Italians ecstatic in the night and the moon, the blue-eyed old woman ecstatic in the busy sunshine, the monks in the garden below, who are supposed to unite both, passing only in the neutrality of the average. Where, then, is the meeting-point: where in mankind is the ecstasy of light and dark together, the supreme transcendence of the afterglow, day hovering in the embrace of the coming night like two angels embracing in the heavens, like Eurydice in the arms of Orpheus, or Persephone embraced by Pluto?

Where is the supreme ecstasy in mankind, which makes day a delight and night a delight, purpose an ecstasy and a concourse in ecstasy, and single abandon of the single body and soul also an ecstasy under the moon? Where is the transcendent knowledge in our hearts, uniting sun and darkness, day and night, spirit and senses? Why do we not know that the two in consummation are one; that each is only part; partial and alone for ever; but that the two in consummation are perfect, beyond the range of loneliness or solitude?

From 'Amanda'

NATHANIEL HOOKES

Sleepie, my Dear? yes, yes, I see
Morpheus is fall'n in love with thee,
Morpheus, my worst of rivals, tries
To draw the Curtains of thine eyes;
And fanns them with his wing asleep,
Makes drowsie love play at hopeep;
How prettily his feathers blow,
Those fleshie shuttings to and fro!
Oh how he makes me Tantalize
With those faire Apples of thine eyes!
Equivocates and cheats me still,
Opening and shutting at his will;
Now both now one, the doting god
Playes with thine eyes at even and odde;

My stamm'ring tongue doubts which it might
Bid thee good-morrow or good-night;
So thy eyes twinkle brighter farre,
Than the bright trembling, ev'ning starre;
So a waxe taper burnt within
The socket playes at out and in.

Index of Titles

Poetry

Index of Authors

Index of First Lines

Prose

Poetry